Castle Dismal;
or, The Bachelor's Christmas

Castle Dismal;
or, The Bachelor's Christmas

William Gilmore Simms

Critical Introduction by
John M. McCardell, Jr. and Brian K. Fennessy
With a Biographical Overview by David Moltke-Hansen

The University of South Carolina Press

Cloth original published by Burgess, Stringer & Co., 1844
Paperback published by the University of South Carolina Press
Columbia, South Carolina 29208

www.sc.edu/uscpress

Manufactured in the United States of America

22 21 20 19 18 17 16 15 14 13
10 9 8 7 6 5 4 3 2 1

ISBN 978-1-61117-261-4 (pbk)

Published in cooperation with the Simms Initiatives, a project of the
University of South Carolina Libraries with the generous support of
the Watson-Brown Foundation, and with additional funding by the
John Govan Simms Endowment.

William Gilmore Simms: A Biographical Overview

David Moltke-Hansen

Introduction

Harper's Weekly put it succinctly in its July 2, 1870, issue: "In the death of Mr. Simms, on the 11th of June, at Charleston, the country has lost one more of its time-honored band of authors, and the South the most consistent and devoted of her literary sons" (qtd. In Butterworth and Kibler 125–26). Indeed no mid-nineteenth-century writer and editor did more than William Gilmore Simms to frame white southern self-identity and nationalism, shape southern histori-cal consciousness, or foster the South's participation and recognition in the broader American literary culture. No southern writer enjoyed more contem-porary esteem and attention, at least after Edgar Allan Poe moved north. Among American romancers (or writers of prose epics), only New Yorker James Fenimore Cooper was as successful by the 1840s. In those same years, Simms was the South's most influential editor of cultural journals. He also was the region's most prolific cultural journalist and poet, publishing an average of one book review and one poem per week for forty-five years.

Before his death Simms saw his national reputation fall along with the Con-federacy he had vigorously supported and with the slave regime that many in the North had come to despise. Nevertheless reprints of most of the twenty titles in the selected edition of his works, first published between 1853 and 1860, appeared up until World War I. Thereafter only *The Yemassee*, an early romance about an Indian war in South Carolina, continued in print. The tide began to turn in the 1950s, when five volumes of Simms's letters appeared and a growing number of his works were issued in new editions. Publication in 1992 of the first literary biography, by John C. Guilds, and establishment of the William Gilmore Simms Society and the *Simms Review* the next year at once reflected and fostered this revived interest. Yet not until the 2011 launch of the digital Simms edition of the South Caroliniana Library of the University of South Carolina did scholars of southern, American, and nineteenth-century culture have the prospect of ready access to all of Simms's separately published works. With the University of South Carolina Press's cooperation, readers also will have access to sixty works in paperback editions by the end of 2014. Simms himself never saw nearly so many of his works in print at one time.

Clearly the decline in the critical standing of, and historical attention to, Simms and his oeuvre in the century after his death has reversed in the years since. The last three decades of the twentieth century saw more published on Simms than the previous hundred years (Butterworth and Kibler 126–200; MLA International). The last decade of the twentieth and first decade of the twenty-first centuries saw more dissertations and theses on him (forty-one) than had appeared in all the years before. This is not to say that Simms is yet given the attention directed to some of his contemporaries. For the first decade of the twenty-first century, the Modern Language Association International Bibliography lists roughly four times as many scholarly publications on James Fenimore Cooper, more than ten times as many on Nathaniel Hawthorne, and sixteen times as many on Edgar Allan Poe. Not surprisingly, therefore, Simms is not yet included in most anthologies of American literature, although he is a subject or a source in an expanding and ever more diverse body of scholarship.

To prepare to read Simms, it is important to see his writings in multiple contexts. He rarely wrote about himself outside of his more personal poems and his letters (some fifteen hundred of the many thousands of which survive). Yet he systematically drew on his background, personal experience, and relationships in his work. He also shaped that work through a progressively developed poetics and philosophy of life, history, and art. He did so in the context of his very broad reading of both contemporary and earlier Western literature and in the midst of multiple professional engagements and responsibilities. The richness and variety of these writings and involvements make Simms a key figure for future understanding of the literary culture, issues, and networks in mid-nineteenth-century America.

Background

Simms's family history reflected the dynamics that fueled the spread southward and westward of the populations, plantation economy, and society of the South Atlantic states. Simms's ancestry also reflected the Scots-Irish and English roots of what became identified as southern culture by the 1830s, a generation after the end of most immigration to the region. Two of Simms's grandparents, William and Elisabeth Sims, were Scots-Irish and migrated to South Carolina from Ulster. One, John Singleton, was an American-born son of putatively English immigrants, who had come to South Carolina from Virginia. The fourth, Jane Miller, was daughter of two Scots-Irish and Irish descended people—John Miller, of North and then South Carolina, and Jane Ross. Ross's family also migrated to South Carolina from western Virginia, where members lived cheek by jowl with other Scots-Irish families, who migrated to the Carolinas (White, *Ross*). Simms's father and Uncle James migrated in 1808 from Charleston to Tennessee, then to Mississippi. This was after the bankruptcy of the elder William's business and the deaths of his wife and their other two sons. Following the last of these losses, the elder Simms's hair turned white in a week. To his anguished eyes, Charleston appeared "a place of tombs" (qtd. in Guilds 6, 12).

For the son, however, Charleston was home—so much so that he refused to leave his maternal grandmother and move to Mississippi when his uncle came to get him in 1816. Then the fifth largest and by far the wealthiest city, as well as one of the greatest ports, in America, Charleston was at the peak of its influence (Moltke-Hansen, "Expansion" 25–31; Rogers). Cotton culture on the sea islands to the south, begun in 1790, and rice culture in impounded lowcountry tidal marshes meant that the port was filled not only with sailors of many lands and languages, but also with enslaved people of many African and Creole cultures and speech ways (slaves continued to be imported legally in large numbers until 1808). This street life made vivid the transnational nature of plantation agriculture and the fact that the developing region's dramatically expanding borders "were not just geographic; they also were human, historical, and intellectual" (Moltke-Hansen, "Southern" 19).

Even more important for the future author, the expanding region's borders and nature were taking imaginative shape. The West of the senior William Gilmore Simms and the first Creek War in which he fought, the Revolutionary War of the young Simms's maternal grandfather, the backcountry of many related Scots-Irish settlers, all these became grist for a lonely, energetic boy, who spent as much time with books as he could (Simms, *Letters* 1:161). The possibilities of such settings, incidents, and characters were not confined to history alone. Simms reported that he "used to glow and shiver in turn over 'The Pilgrim's Progress,'" while "Moses' adventures in 'The Vicar of Wakefield' threw [him] into paroxysms of laughter" (Hayne 261–62). Sir Walter Scott's Border and medieval romances and James Fenimore Cooper's Leatherstocking tales also deeply colored his imagination (Simms, *Views* 1:248, and Moltke-Hansen, "Southern" 6–15). As affecting were the ghost stories and Revolutionary War tales of his grandmother and the verses sent, and tales told, by his father.

These diverse tales became reasons to explore—in books, but also on the ground. As a boy, Simms ranged through the city and along the banks of the Ashley River, which fed into Charleston Harbor. He did so in search of scenes of colonial and Revolutionary battles and incidents (*Letters* 1:lxii). He first heard his uncle's and father's many Irish and frontier stories when they visited in Charleston in 1816 and 1818, respectively. He heard more on his trips to Mississippi during the winter of 1824 through the spring of 1825 and again in 1826. The first trip took him through Georgia and Alabama, where he saw elements of the Creek and Cherokee nations. At the time, Simms later reported, he was a boy "cumbered with fragmentary materials of thought, . . . choked by the tangled vines of erroneous speculation, and haunted by passions, which, like so many wolves, lurked, in ready waiting, for their unsuspecting prey" (*Social* 6). When he first got to Mississippi, traveling partly by stage, partly by riverboat, and partly by horse, Simms learned that his father had just come back from "a trip of three hundred miles into the heart of the Indian country" (Trent 15). Later father and son "rode together on horseback to various settlements on the frontier of Alabama and Mississippi" (Guilds 10–11, 17–18). Simms recalled as well "having traveled 150 miles beyond the Mississippi" (Shillingsburg, "Literary Grist" 120). The next year he returned to the Southwest by ship. "During this [second] trip he carried a 'note book.'" There he jotted episodes, encounters, stories heard, characters seen, and descriptions of the landscapes unfolding around him. He also wrote "at least sixteen poems" (Kibler, "First"; Shillingsburg, "Literary Grist" 123).

Simms took a third western trip five years later, writing letters back to the newspaper that by then he was editing (*Letters* 1:10–38). Together these three trips provided materials for his writings over more than forty years. "The first . . . produced mainly short fiction; the second inspired much poetry; . . . the first and third . . . yielded three novels written in the 1830s" (Shillingsburg, "Literary Grist" 119). This was, in part, because of the trips' timing. Sixteen years after the first trip, Simms told students at the University of Alabama that in the interval their world had changed from a howling wilderness into a place of growing civilization (Simms, *Social* 5–6). Had he not gone when he did, he would have been too late to see the frontier. Later travels took him many other places and also provided much grist for his writing. Never again, however, did he experience the frontier firsthand. Furthermore, on these later trips Simms was a practiced professional writer, no longer that boy haunted by passions.

Personal Life

After the ten-year-old boy's momentous refusal to leave Charleston, his grandmother sent Simms for two years to the grammar school taught on the campus and by the faculty of the nearly moribund College of Charleston. By then he already was "versifying the events of the war [of 1812]," just concluded, publishing "doggerel" in the local papers, and learning to read in several languages (*Letters* 1:285). His trip west a decade later helped him decide to pursue both literature and a career in law, but back in Charleston—this despite his father's urging that he stay in Mississippi. Upon his return home, he began to read law and also launched a literary weekly, the *Album*, which ran for a year. He became engaged as well to Anna Malcolm Giles, daughter of a grocer and former state coroner.

A year later the young couple married. This was six months before Simms was admitted to the South Carolina bar, on his twenty-first birthday, not long before he was appointed as a city magistrate. Although living up the Ashley River in the more healthful, less expensive village of Summerville, Simms kept a law office in the city. Shortly after using his maternal inheritance to buy the *City Gazette* at the end of 1829 and moving down to Charleston Neck, just north of the city limits where he had lived as a boy, Simms lost both his father and his maternal grandmother. He also found himself attacked because of his Unionist stance in the Nullification crisis resulting from South Carolina's rejection of a federal tariff. Then, in early 1832, Simms's wife died. Soon after, he took his four-year-old daughter back to Summerville to live and determined to sell his newspaper and leave the state for a literary life in the North.

Fueling his ambition was the correspondence Simms had begun several years earlier with an accountant whom he had published in his *City Gazette* but not yet met—Scots immigrant James Lawson. At the time Lawson, seven years Simms's senior, edited a New York City newspaper and, in addition to writing plays and poetry, was a friend (and, later, informal literary agent) to a wide circle (McHaney, "An Early"). Simms's trip north in the summer of 1832 saw the two begin a lifelong friendship, cemented as they squired ladies about and interacted with Lawson's literary circle. In subsequent years Simms multiplied the number of his friendships, in both the North and the South, making them in some measure a replacement for the family that he had lost. Lawson remained the closest of his northern friends, while James Henry Hammond, a future governor and U.S. senator, became his closest friend in South Carolina.

Late in 1833, after his Summerville house burned, Simms wrote Lawson to say that he was enamored of "a certain fair one" (*Letters* 1:73). Seventeen-year-old Chevillette Eliza Roach was the daughter of "a literary-minded aristocrat of English descent" with two plantations on the banks of the Edisto River in Barnwell District (later County) (Guilds 70). The courtship was protracted, as Simms felt it necessary first to clear debts that friends had bought up on his behalf. He also was determined "to marry no woman" before he was "perfectly independent of her resources, and her friends" (*Letters* 1:78). Therefore he did not propose until the spring of 1836. The nuptials took place seven months later, and as a result, Simms came to call the four thousand acres of Woodlands Plantation, with its seventy slaves, home. It was twenty years, however, before he took over management of the plantation and, then, only in the wake of his father-in-law's final sickness and death. Five years after that, he lost his wife, the mother of fourteen of his fifteen children. Nine of the children Chevillette bore him had already died, devastating Simms repeatedly. Five were still living (three sons and two daughters), as was Simms's daughter by his first marriage, who helped raise the youngest of her siblings. Those remaining children—even Gilly, who fought in the Confederate army—all outlived their father. Gilly and a brother-in-law ran Woodlands after the war, when Simms, though dying of cancer, was earning what he could by writing again for publications in the North and editing one or another South Carolina newspaper.

Career

The trip north in 1832 did not result in Simms moving there. Except during the Civil War, however, he returned almost every year. This was because the contacts he made, and the exposure to literary culture that he enjoyed, helped him define his future as an author. Earlier he had written fiction and criticism as well as journalism, filling the pages of several short-lived cultural journals and his newspaper, but between the ages of nine and twenty-six Simms had focused his literary efforts primarily on poetry. Beginning with his first book of verse in 1825, he had published five small volumes in Charleston. A couple had received positive notice in New York, and in the fall of 1832, J. & J. Harper issued the sixth anonymously from there, *Atalantis: A Story of the Sea*. Coming back the following summer, Simms had in hand for the Harpers a gothic novella, *Martin Faber*, and after his return south, he also would send the manuscript of his first two-volume border romance, *Guy Rivers: A Tale of Georgia*.

The reception of these and the romances and short stories that followed quickly made Simms one of the nation's most successful fictionists. He continued to issue poetry as well—roughly a collection every three years over the thirty-seven years that he worked as a professional author. But this output was dwarfed by the fiction—on average a title every year (counting several serialized works but not counting the many revised editions). Then there were the two dozen separately published orations, histories, and biographies as well as edited collections of documents and dramas and a geography of South Carolina. Add to these the revised editions and the further printings and issues of his own works and it appears that Simms saw a title coming off the presses at the rate of one every three months or so. Making that figure all the more astounding is the fact that, during more than a dozen of those years (the early-to-mid 1840s, the late 1840s-to-early 1850s, and the mid-to-late 1860s), he also was editing a cultural journal or newspaper. Furthermore he contributed reams of reviews and poems, hundreds of op-ed pieces and columns, and dozens of short stories and public addresses, which were never collected and published in volume form.

His career mapped an arc. It ascended meteorically in the 1830s and peaked in the early-to-mid 1840s, before beginning to descend. One reason was the popularity of the historical fiction that Simms began to write. When he left behind the law, his first newspaper, and the Nullification controversy, as well as his sadness, historical fiction was all the rage. Sir Walter Scott had fueled the craze, beginning with the publication of his first Border romance in 1814. He died in September 1832. Seventeen years Simms's senior, James Fenimore Cooper, the closest America had to a Scott at the time, was at the peak of his reputation and success, having started publishing his romances in 1820. Thus the way had been prepared for a writer of Simms's historical imagination and preoccupations. Within five years of his first trip north, moreover, Lawson's (and now his) circle became loosely affiliated with a nationalistic and Democratic group, self-styled Young America, this after Young Italy and similar ethnic, nationalist, European, cultural and political movements (Moltke-Hansen, "Southern"). Edgar Allan Poe and other members gave Simms's first fictions positive, if not uncritical, attention.

By the end of the 1830s, paradoxically, Simms, like Cooper, found his success attracting unauthorized editions of his works because Britain and America did not have an international copyright agreement. Further, in the wake of the panic of 1837, Americans bought fewer books. Simms's response was to diversify his portfolio. He turned to biography and history, including his hugely successful *Life of Francis Marion* (1844). He also returned to the editor's chair, overseeing one and then another cultural journal. These were unlike the ones he had edited in the 1820s: they included contributions by numerous authors, not just those from Charleston, but from the region and also the North. The ambition motivating the journals was to connect and promote Charleston intellectually. Consequently the journals more closely resembled metropolitan quarterly reviews in their offerings.

The mid-1840s saw Simms involved in politics, even serving a term in the South Carolina legislature. By the middle of the Mexican-American War in 1847, he had concluded that the South needed to become an independent nation. Thereafter, although he maintained ties with many in the Young America circle, he no longer promoted his writings as fostering Americanism in literature (*Views*). Instead he increasingly emphasized the ways in which his three romance series — the colonial, the Revolutionary, and the border — were making tangible and meaningful the origins and development of the future southern nation and the sad but inevitable consequences for Native Americans (Watson, *From Nationalism*; compare Nakamura).

Sectional politics colored more and more of Simms's perceptions, speeches, and private communications. The rising tide of abolitionism had him aghast. It also fed his growing sense that his position in American letters was slipping. He returned to editing, and his poetry, which was more often explicitly about the South, became increasingly patriotic in tone. Although his first biographer, William Peterfield Trent, insisted that Simms's declining standing reflected the change in literary fashion from historical romances to realistic novels, Simms in fact wrote more and more as a social realist in the 1850s (Wimsatt, "Realism").

The Civil War consumed Simms. As he wrote Lawson, "Literature, especially poetry, is effectually overwhelmed by the drums, & the cavalry, and the shouting" (*Letters* 4:369–70). He did manage to editorialize often and to rework and finish things long on his desk, including poems, a novel, and a dramatic treatment of Benedict Arnold, the northern traitor in the Revolutionary War. Then, in the wake of the Confederacy's loss and the failure of his vision for the South, he found himself recording the loss in a new newspaper, dealing with the trauma in his poetry, and becoming more existential and psychological in his fictional treatments. Simms's old New York friends tried to help. He did edit and see through publication a volume of Confederate war poetry. Yet it is a measure of his reduced stature that the several new romances he published appeared only in serial form. In part this may have been because he was in a sense competing with himself. Publishers were beginning to reprint volumes out of the selected edition of his writings. Many of Simms's works were available in book form, just not new works.

Associations

As the *Letters* testify, Simms had complex, overlapping networks of friends and colleagues. As a boy and young man, he received the friendship, patronage, and commendation of a variety of well-placed people in Charleston, including Charles Rivers Carroll. It was Carroll with whom he read law, to whom he dedicated his first romance, and after whom he named a son. Both men were Unionists during the Nullification controversy. So were Hugh Swinton Legare (later U.S. attorney general) and the considerably older William Drayton, as well as lawyer and editor Richard Yeadon and Greenville, South Carolina, newspaper editor Benjamin Franklin Perry. Also considerably older was James Wright Simmons, who had joined with Simms to launch the *Southern Literary Gazette* in 1828, when Simms was twenty-two. Through him Simms had direct contact with such British literary figures as Leigh Hunt and Byron (Kibler, *Poetry* 15).

The next group of influential friends and collaborators that Simms acquired were members of the Lawson circle and included such figures as Edwin

Forrest, the Shakespearean actor, and Evert Duyckinck, who published several of Simms's volumes in Wiley and Putnam's series Library of American Books, which he edited. Among the many others were poets and editors William Cullen Bryant and Fitz-Greene Halleck. Simms also made nonliterary friends in New York and Philadelphia, such as John Jacob Bockee and William Hawkins Ferris, the cashier at the U.S. Treasury office in New York who, after the war, helped Simms, Henry Timrod (poet laureate of the Confederacy), and others.

As a Barnwell planter, Simms met a widening circle of South Carolina's leaders and literati. For instance his acquaintance with James Henry Hammond began in the late 1830s and deepened into a friendship in the early 1840s. It was in the early 1840s, too, when he again was editing cultural journals, that Simms became friends with many southern writers. He regarded several of them, including Virginians George Frederick Holmes, Edmund Ruffin, and Nathaniel Beverley Tucker as members, together with Hammond and himself, in a "sacred circle." Uniting the circle were members' devotion to the South and a shared sense of the marginal status and critical importance of the life of the mind in a largely rural and unintellectual region (Faust, *Sacred*). Others of Simms's wide connections in the region did not interact as much with each other, but Simms long corresponded with Maryland novelist and lawyer John Pendleton Kennedy, Irish-born Georgia poet Richard Henry Wilde, Alabama lawyer and writer Alexander Beaufort Meek, and Louisiana historian and assistant attorney general Charles Gayarré, among others. By the 1850s, when Simms once more returned to editing a cultural journal, many of the writers whom he recruited were members of a younger generation. Poets Paul Hamilton Hayne and Henry Timrod were two. Often they and a half dozen others of Simms's and their generations met in John Russell's Charleston Book Shop and adjourned to dinner at Simms's Smith Street home, "dubbed 'The Wigwam'" (*Letters* 1:cxxxvi). Shortly before his death fifteen or so years later, Simms wrote Hayne, "I am rapidly passing from the stage, where you young men are to succeed me" (*Letters* 5:287).

Thought

The welter of Simms's works disguises unities and dynamics of the thought underlying them. From early on Simms was convinced that art ennobles or transforms, as well as gives voice to individuals and societies; therefore it must be cultivated assiduously. Without the potential for high artistic attainment, he insisted, societies are not ready for the independence and regard of free peoples. This is where Simms the historian joined Simms the poet. Societies develop, he argued (using the stadialism of the Scottish historical school), from imitation through self-assertion to achievement and also from savagery through strife to settled agricultural communities and, ultimately, to a hierarchical civilization supporting a rich artistic life. It was the job of the artist to help envision the goal, inspire the pursuit, and inform the process. That process was at once progressive and dialectical. Order, without dynamism, stifled development, as did the obverse—the dominance by ungoverned impulses or uncontrolled license. This was true in the individual, but also in societies as a whole. War was necessary for civilization, but its success was measured in the securities of the home, the center of cultural production and reproduction.

Whether in the public or in the domestic arena, "the true governor, as [Thomas] Carlyle call[ed] him—the king man—" guided rather than impeded the forces of change and progress (Simms, "Guizot's" 122). There were few such men with the capacity to lead. The same was true of nations. Neither all people nor all peoples were equal in either capacity or attainment. That was why Native Americans were overrun and Africans had been enslaved by European peoples in the New World. Indeed, Simms argued, "slavery in all ages has been found the greatest and most admirable agent of Civilization," giving education and examples to less evolved peoples (*Letters* 3:174). The degree to which a people had evolved mattered. That was why, he held, Americans had won independence from the most powerful empire in the world. They had done so through their Revolution, led by an elite that felt correctly its time had come (Simms, "Ellet's" 328). By mid-1847 that also was Simms's judgment for the South: the region had evolved enough to become independent (*Letters* 2:332). The hope inspired and then failed him and the people he sought to lead.

While not all men could rise to the highest rank, they all had the same responsibility at home. There the father was patriarch, protector, and head, while the mother was nurturer, moral instructor, and heart. There, too, children's characters and minds were formed by age twelve ("Ellet's"). Children's upbringing was critical to citizenship, and it was through her sons and the support of her husband, father, and brothers that a woman shaped the public sphere. The culture and character instilled in the child expressed and informed not just the household, but the larger society—the people.

"The history of peoples and their embodiments in institutions, states, and artistic productions—these were the great subjects" in Simms's view (Moltke-Hansen, "Southern" 120). Yet "poets were the only class of philosophers who had recognized" this until his own day, when at last "we now read human histories. We now ask after the affections as well as the ceremonies of society" ("Ellet's" 319–20). Peoples or races—that is, ethnic groups—were not unchanging any more than were their politics and their cultures. They either advanced or were overrun by history. Further, new peoples emerged, and old identities were submerged. The Spanish conquistadors were the creation of centuries of conflict with the Moors: their motivation was the glory of conquest, not the routine of trade or the plow. On the other hand, the English settlements in North America reflected the impulse to transform the wilderness into verdant farms and build society (*Views* 64, 178–85; *Social* 8). The same impulse drove Americans westward in Simms's own day and gave Americans their Manifest Destiny.

To explore these facts of the South's settlement and its place in international conflicts, Simms wrote all together, between 1833 and 1863, two romances set in eighth-century Spain, two set during the Spanish exploration and conquest of the Americas and two during the later English colonization of South Carolina, seven set during the American Revolution, and — depending on how one counts — perhaps eight set on the borders of the nineteenth-century South. After the war he published one more Revolutionary romance and two more that, like it, were set beyond the boundaries of civilization. He also left two unfinished romances, also set beyond society's normal reach. These late works, however, no longer had as their framing justification the cultivation of the South's future and civilization.

White southerners had their independence foreclosed by the war. In his last works, therefore, Simms found himself exploring the psychological, philosophical, and historical impulses that led to the Confederacy's demise and what, in the aftermath, it meant to be a good man and to build for the future, however impoverished. On the first score, he argued that the impulse to idealism behind abolitionism ignored historical realities, becoming inhuman in its consequences. On the latter score, he affirmed responsibility for one's dependents and the virtues of stoicism, as well as a continued commitment to the beauty and truth of art and the impulses to the cultivated life and fields. Therefore, in the face of the burning of his Woodlands home and library in February 1865 — during Sherman's march and in the midst of desperate circumstances — he insisted that home, or the ideals and past characterizing its potential, still was at the center of true civilization, but only if elevated by art (*Sense* 8, 17). It was wrong to measure civilization by the getting, spending, and mad dashing, or material progress and utilitarianism, characteristic of both a capitalistic North and also many southerners. These traits he often had attacked even before the war, insisting that "the work of the Imagination, which is the Genius of a race, is only begun when its material progress is supposed to be complete" (*Poetry* 12).

Writings

Simms expressed many of his ideas most personally in letters and most cogently in essays, speeches, and occasional introductions to his books. But he illustrated them most fully in his fiction and poetry. By the time he arrived in New

York in 1832, he had formed many of the core ideals and beliefs that would shape his work. His application of them, however, modified his understanding over time. Growing as a writer and growing in knowledge and experience, he also grew as a thinker.

In his hierarchy of values, poetry came first. It was a prophetic calling as well as evocative of the deeply felt (or, sometimes, the fleeting) and thus testimony to the perdurance and transcendence of the beautiful and the human spirit. Yet, as Simms often ruefully reflected, prose spoke to many more people. That was a principal reason why he turned to writing prose epics or romances. He gave his most concerted consideration of poetry's value and roles in three lectures in Charleston in 1854. Over the prior three years he had given portions of them in Augusta, Georgia, Washington, D.C., and Richmond and Petersburg, Virginia. Entitled *Poetry and the Practical*, they did not see print until 1996, as Simms never found the time to expand them as he wanted. On the other hand, his last address on the same themes, *The Sense of the Beautiful*, was issued soon after he delivered it, also in Charleston.

Many of his important reviews have not yet been gathered, but Simms collected some in 1845–46, and *Views and Reviews in American Literature, History and Fiction* came out in 1846 and 1847 in two "series." Beginning with a consideration of "Americanism" in literature, the first series explored the themes and periods of American history for treatment by the novelist. Simms argued there, and in forewords to several of his romances, that fiction rendered the past more truthfully, interestingly, and tellingly than histories and biographies could because fiction — like poetry — required imagination to look beyond what is not known or expressed. The second series examined additional American writers and what distinguished them, for instance, in their humor.

Despite their early success, Simms's romances, novellas, and stories provoked mixed reviews. Poe eventually concluded that Simms had become "the best novelist which this country has, on the whole, produced" but also insisted that "he should never have written 'The Partisan,' nor 'The Yemassee.'" This was in a review of *Confession*. That novel, like the gothic *Martin Faber*, demonstrated, Poe contended, that Simms's "genius [did] not lie in the outward so much as in the inner world." Yet he nevertheless wrote of Simms's short-story collection *The Wigwam and the Cabin* that "in invention, in vigor, in movement, in the power of exciting interest, and in the artistical management of his themes, he has surpassed, we think, any of his countrymen." Other critics, especially in the genteel and Whiggish Knickerbocker circle, joined Poe in condemning what they considered to be the excessively graphic and vulgar qualities of many characters and scenes, and Simms's prolixity and sententiousness, in his romances (Butterworth and Kibler 64, 50).

The violent realism and earthiness of the romances did not result in realistic novels. Although Simms received early praise for his characterizations (particularly of women), he used the romance formula, with its stereotypic heroes and heroines, predictable themes, and conventional polarities. People were on quests or had lost their way or were fighting long odds or were carrying forward the banner of (and modeling) civilization or were mired in the slough of despond or were resisting all the claims of civilized society and behavior or were pursuing love interests. Deceitfulness, selfishness, and greed opposed honor, high-mindedness, and honesty against the backdrop of the South's development from the earliest days of Spanish exploration to the westward movement in Simms's own youth.

It was only gradually that Simms married the psychological acuity of some of his portraits of the interior struggles of his gothic characters and fiction to the historical romance. Helping him think through how to do so were the biographies he wrote in the mid-1840s, but also the incidents on which he focused particular fictions, such as the murder in *Beauchampe; or, The Kentucky Tragedy* (1842). However incomplete the blending of realism and romanticism or of stereotypical and socially individuated renderings through the 1840s, by the 1850s Simms fundamentally had made the transition to social realism in such works as *Woodcraft* and *The Cassique of Kiawah*. Indeed some scholars have considered *Woodcraft* the first realistic novel in America (Bakker; Wimsatt, "Realism").

In some sense disguising the transition is the fact that Simms also increasingly wrote as a humorist and, in so doing, often rendered his late narratives fabulistically, when not writing social comedy or stories of manners. This dimension of Simms's work was largely hidden, however, until the 1974 publication of *Stories and Tales*, volume 5 in the Centennial Simms edition. There, for the first time, readers had access in print to "Bald-Head Bill Bauldy." There, too, for the first time one could read together that story, "Legend of the Hunter's Camp," and "How Sharp Snaffles Got His Capital and Wife," which was published posthumously in *Harper's Magazine* in October 1870. These and other stories and tales made it clear that Simms was a fecund contributor to southern and American humor.

Humor let Simms take up issues that he could not otherwise address in print and still expect to be well received. He did so both during and after the war. The war also pushed Simms past the emerging fashion of social realism. Having destroyed the familiar, the preoccupation of much realistic fiction, the war made the liminal central (Shillingsburg, "Cub"). While his romances and tales had often explored life on the edge or in extreme circumstances, whether in war or on the frontier or on the verge of madness or in fanciful realms, it had done so against a backdrop of, and with the goal of affirming, social norms and development. In the war's wake that goal seemed absurd. Mythologized memories of a healthy past might nurture a sense of the beautiful but could not help one deal with the present. Thus Simms's conclusion, in a March 1869 letter to Paul Hamilton Hayne: "Let us bury the Past lest it buries us!" (*Letters* 5:214). Fifteen months later he lay dead in the 13 Society Street, Charleston, home of his oldest daughter, with the shell holes in the walls of the bedroom he had shared with several children.

Posthumous Reputation

The twenty years after Simms's death saw him often respectfully treated, first in obituaries, later in memoirs and columns, and also in literary dictionaries and encyclopedias. Yet Charles Richardson's 1887 *American Literature: 1607–1885* proved a harbinger of a shift: Simms, Richardson observed, was "more respected than read," having "won considerable note because he was so sectional" and then having "lost it because he was not sectional enough," although he showed "silly contempt for his Northern betters" (qtd. in Butterworth and Kibler 130). Five years later Trent's biography of Simms appeared. It was the first full-length, scholarly treatment. Its central thesis was that Simms's environment frustrated his abilities: the South was inimical to art and the life of the mind, and Charleston high society's hauteur marginalized Simms despite his talent and character. Trent's second thesis was that Simms's commitment to the romance and his romanticism meant that his works had become largely unreadable in an age of literary realism. Although Vernon Parrington and later scholars recognized Simms's impulses to realism, the two theses long shaped Simms criticism and, indeed, also helped frame study of antebellum southern literature and intellectual life (Parrington 119–30).

A Virginian born in 1862, Trent was a progressive who wanted a New South radically different from the old. He saw his pioneering study of Simms as an opportunity to criticize what the Civil War had made untenable. From his perspective the Old South was not the expanding and rapidly developing environment, with a deep history, that Simms portrayed, but a place where slavery stultified and stunted the growth and progress displayed by the North. Southern—especially South Carolinian—writers occasionally challenged Trent's agenda and conclusions, but those critiques had little impact. Not until after publication of the Simms letters in the 1950s did scholars begin to consider the author in the historical and contemporary contexts that he had rendered in his poetry and fiction. And not until after the centennial of his death did a growing number of scholars, having concluded that southern intellectual history was

not an oxymoron, begin to study in detail the culture in which Simms partici-
pated and to which he contributed so voluminously and variously.

Some of these scholars also have had agendas: they have wanted to see
Simms included in the American literary canon, for instance, or they have
wanted to defend the heritage that in their view Trent, and so many others,
inappropriately belittled or ignorantly dismissed. More fruitfully, other scholars have begun to reframe the understanding of nineteenth-century American
intellectual life by stripping away preconceptions that characterized earlier
evaluations of Simms and his contemporaries. They are closely examining the
historical record and transatlantic and other contemporary contexts and devel-
opments in the process. Although the pursuit of canonical status in a post-
canonical age seems quixotic at this point, the explosion of the canon is leading
to more varied fare being offered and may, therefore, mean that Simms, once
his work is widely available, will be more often anthologized as well as studied. Defensiveness about Simms and the antebellum South may warm the
hearts of like-minded people, just as critics of the Old South have been encouraged by shared presuppositions and disdain. Yet dueling cultural ideologies do
not advance comity and may only reinforce mutual incomprehensions. Continued, deep research in original sources and the theoretical reframing that
Atlantic history, the history of the book, and other perspectives offer — these
approaches promise most for further study of Simms, his works, and his world.

Works Cited

For amplified readings by and on Simms and on his world, go to http://simms.library
.sc.edu/bibliography.php.

Bakker, Jan. "Simms on the Literary Frontier; or, So Long Miss Ravenel and Hello Cap-
tain Porgy: *Woodcraft* Is the First 'Realistic' Novel in America." In *William Gilmore
Simms and the American Frontier*, edited by John Caldwell Guilds and Caroline Collins,
64–78. Athens: University of Georgia Press, 1997.
Butterworth, Keen, and James E. Kibler Jr. *William Gilmore Simms: A Definitive Guide.*
Boston: G. K. Hall, 1980.
Faust, Drew Gilpin. *A Sacred Circle: The Dilemma of the Intellectual in the Old South, 1840–
1860.* Baltimore: Johns Hopkins University Press, 1977.
Guilds, John C. *Simms: A Literary Life.* Fayetteville: University of Arkansas Press, 1992.
Hayne, Paul Hamilton. "Ante-Bellum Charleston." *Southern Bivouac* 1 (October 1885):
257–68.
Kibler, James E. "The First Simms Letters: 'Letters from the West' (1826)." *Southern Liter-
ary Journal* 19 (Spring 1987): 81–91.
———. *The Poetry of William Gilmore Simms: An Introduction and Bibliography.* Columbia:
Southern Studies Program, University of South Carolina, 1979.

McHaney, Thomas L. "An Early 19th-Century Literary Agent: James Lawson of New York." *Publications of the Bibliographical Society of America* 64 (Spring 1970): 177–92.

Moltke-Hansen, David. "The Expansion of Intellectual Life: A Prospectus." In *Intellectual Life in Antebellum Charleston,* edited by Michael O'Brien and David Moltke-Hansen, 3–44. Knoxville: University of Tennessee Press, 1986.

———. "Southern Literary Horizons in Young America: Imaginative Development of a Regional Geography." *Studies in the Literary Imagination* 42, no. 1 (2009): 1–31.

Nakamura, Masahiro. *Visions of Order in William Gilmore Simms: Southern Conservatism and the Other American Romance.* Columbia: University of South Carolina Press, 2009.

Parrington, Vernon L. *The Romantic Revolution in America, 1800–1860.* Vol. 2 of *Main Currents in American Thought.* New York: Harcourt, Brace and Company, 1927.

Rogers, George C., Jr. *Charleston in the Age of the Pinckneys.* Columbia: University South Carolina Press, 1980.

Shillingsburg, Miriam J. "The Cub of the Panther: A New Frontier." In *William Gilmore Simms and the American Frontier,* edited by John Caldwell Guilds and Caroline Collins, 221–36. Athens: University of Georgia Press, 1997.

———. "Literary Grist: Simms's Trips to Mississippi." *Southern Quarterly* 41, no. 2 (2003): 119–34.

Simms, William Gilmore. *Atalantis: A Story of the Sea: In Three Parts.* New York: J. & J. Harper, 1832.

———. *Beauchampe; or, The Kentucky Tragedy.* 2 vols. Philadelphia: Lea and Blanchard, 1842.

———. *The Cassique of Kiawah: A Colonial Romance.* New York: Redfield, 1859.

———. *Confession; or, The Blind Heart. A Domestic Story.* 2 vols. Philadelphia: Lea and Blanchard, 1841.

———. "Ellet's 'Women of the Revolution.'" *Southern Quarterly Review,* n.s. 1 (July 1850): 314–54.

———. "Guizot's Democracy in France." *Southern Quarterly Review* 15, no.29 (1849): 114–65.

———. *Guy Rivers: A Tale of Georgia.* 2 vols. New York: Harper & Brothers, 1834.

———. *The Letters of William Gilmore Simms.* Edited by Mary C. Simms Oliphant, Alfred Taylor Odell, and T. C. Duncan. 6 vols. Columbia: University of South Carolina Press, 1952–82.

———. *The Life of Francis Marion.* New York: Henry G. Langley, 1844.

———. *Martin Faber, the Story of a Criminal; and Other Tales.* 2 vols. New York: Harper & Brothers, 1837.

———. *Poetry and the Practical.* Edited by James E. Kibler. Fayetteville: University of Arkansas Press, 1996.

———. *The Sense of the Beautiful: An Address . . . before the Charleston County Agricultural and Horticultural Association, May 3, 1870.* Charleston: Charleston County Agricultural and Horticultural Association, 1870.

———. *The Social Principle: The Source of National Permanence. An Oration, Delivered before the Erosophic Society of the University of Alabama . . . December 13, 1842.* Tuscaloosa: Erosophic Society, University of Alabama, 1843.

———. *Stories and Tales.* Vol. 5 of *The Writings of William Gilmore Simms.* Centennial edition; introductions, explanatory notes, and texts established by John Caldwell Guilds. Columbia: University of South Carolina Press, 1974.

———. *Views and Reviews in American Literature, History and Fiction.* 2 vols. New York: Wiley and Putnam, 1845 (1846).

———. *The Wigwam and the Cabin.* 2 vols. New York: Wiley and Putnam, 1845–46.

———. *Woodcraft, or Hawks about the Dovecote: A Story of the South, at the Close of the Revolution.* New York: Redfield, 1854.

Trent, William Peterfield. *William Gilmore Simms.* Boston: Houghton, Mifflin, 1892.

Wakelyn, Jon L. *The Politics of a Literary Man: William Gilmore Simms.* Westport, Conn.: Greenwood Press, 1973.

Watson, Charles S. *From Nationalism to Secessionism: The Changing Fiction of William Gilmore Simms.* Westport, Conn.: Greenwood Press, 1993.

White, William B., Jr. *The Ross-Chesnut-Sutton Family of South Carolina.* Franklin, N.C.: Privately printed, 2002.

Wimsatt, Mary Ann. "Realism and Romance in Simms's Midcentury Fiction." *Southern Literary Journal* 12, no. 2 (1980): 29–48.

Critical Introduction

CASTLE DISMAL

John M. McCardell, Jr. and Brian K. Fennessy

"I have been scribbling another story," wrote William Gilmore Simms in early January 1841, "called 'Castle Dismal, or a Bachelor's Christmas in Carolina.'" The Christmas season had just concluded at "Woodlands," the plantation where Simms and his family resided from the first frost of November through late May. As the new year dawned Simms, at 34 already an accomplished editor, poet, novelist, and critic, described, in a long letter to his New York friend and regular correspondent, James Lawson, his most recent achievements and his latest plans. A novel *The Kinsmen; or, the Black Riders of the Congaree*, was to be published in February. A short story, "Murder Will Out," had been sent off to "Miss Leslie" for publication in *The Gift*. Another story, "The Muse of the Ballet," was under review for publication in *Godey's*. A series of essays, accurately described by Simms as "very scorching & searching," on the topic "Southern Literature," had begun to appear in the monthly magazine *Magnolia* in December and would continue for three more installments (*Letters* 1: 209-13).

Indeed, Simms was in the midst of an enormously productive period. In 1840, the year just past, he had published a series of poems in the *Southern Literary Messenger* and *Godey's* and an "Apostrophe to Ocean" in the *Democratic Review*. He had published, to enthusiastic reviews, his *History of South Carolina*. For six weeks in June and July, after settling his family in Charleston for the summer, he had visited New York for the first time in three years. There he saw Lawson, met with publishers, and renewed acquaintances with that city's lively artistic and literary community. He had en route stopped for brief visits in Washington, Baltimore, and Philadelphia. In November his agricultural oration at Barnwell Courthouse evoked a demand that it be published and also suggested that the orator might have a future in politics (*Letters* 1: 170-71).

The preceding twelve months, in other words, had shown all of Simms's protean talents on display. And his energy and creativity did not appear to be flagging. He continued to write and publish poetry, to compose essays and stories, to make notes for proposed biographies of "worthies of Carolina Revolutionary History," and even to try his hand at drama. He concluded his letter to Lawson by requesting back copies of *Knickerbocker* magazine and newly published anthologies of poetry, edited by George Pope Morris and William Cullen Bryant, the latter including two of Simms's works. Hoping, as always, for a prompt response in the form of "a budget of personal & literary news to enliven me," Simms sealed the letter and returned to his literary labors (*Letters* 1: 213).

The past year of activity, and that in which Simms now found himself engaged, offered revealing suggestions about his temperament, his work habits, his remarkable range of interests and, also, why, to so many critics over so many years, the most accurate assessment of his status as an American author has remained his own self-composed epitaph: "Here lies one, who after a reasonably long life, distinguished chiefly by unceasing labor, has left all his better works undone" ("Personal").

I.

"Castle Dismal," published under the pseudonym G.B. Singleton, appeared in monthly installments in *Magnolia*, beginning in January 1842. No chapter appeared in May. The editors explained the hiatus as simply a decision "to defer the publication of the Sixth Chapter ... in order to conclude that of 'Turgesius,'" a Viking chief who plundered Ireland in 832 A.D. ("Editorial" 320). Doubtless readers were on the edge of their seats to learn how this came out.

Though the story resumed in June, it was preceded by distressing news:

> An unexpected and grievous domestic calamity in the family of Mr. Simms — the loss of his youngest daughter — deprives us, to a certain extent, of his assistance in the present number, and will no doubt abridge considerably the amount of his labours for that ensuing. This event impairs several of the literary and other arrangements of our work, but we trust that the interruption ... will be only temporary ("Editorial" 320).

Indeed, Simms was shattered by the sudden loss. "In the moment of my greatest seeming security, when everything was calm around me," he lamented to his friend James Henry Hammond, "the bolt fell at my fireside." Mary Derrille Simms, 2 ½ years old, succumbed to scarlet fever in late April 1842. "Of four [children] I have but one left," he continued, adding, significantly, "of the 3 children of my present wife not one .... I am almost wholly baffled and broken up (*Letters* 1: 303-04)."

The "present wife" of whom Simms spoke was his second. He had married, first, Anna Malcolm Giles, of Charleston, in 1826, and she had borne him a daughter, Anna Augusta Singleton. But Anna died, and, in 1836, Simms remarried, this time to Chevillette Roach, age 18. Chevillette was the daughter of Nash Roach, a planter with two plantations in Barnwell District. By this marriage Simms, age 30, had become a member of the planter class. For the rest of his life "Woodlands," one of the two Roach plantations, would be his beloved home (*Letters* 1: lxvi-lxviii, lxxvii). Yet, in 1842, that home was devastated. All three children by Chevillette had died. Simms, clearly, was undone.

When the *Magnolia* noted the most recent of these deaths, it also mentioned "literary and other arrangements" referring to Simms's agreement, in March 1842, to take over as editor of that publication and move its offices from Savannah to Charleston (Guilds 134). The fifth installment of "Castle Dismal" appeared in the June 1842 issue. The sixth and final chapter never was published.

Editorial demands and family grief undoubtedly delayed completion of the story as well as its revision for publication as a book. Simms sailed from Charleston to New York on 31 July 1843. He returned to Charleston in mid-September and soon after forwarded to Lawson the finished manuscript of "William Potter, or a Christmas at Castle Dismal — a Ghost Story," which he asked Lawson to deliver to the Harpers for publication (*Letters* 1: 363). Thus, it is clear that by the end of September 1843 Simms had completed the hitherto incomplete tale and had also made revisions to the *Magnolia* version.

The Harpers declined to publish, and there was likewise little interest among other of Simms's and Lawson's contacts. Finally, in February 1844, increasingly concerned to get the story "off my hands without positively giving [it] away" (*Letters* 1: 404), Simms asked Lawson to deliver the story to Burgess and Stringer, a new publishing house that had also secured the rights to James Fenimore Cooper's works. Burgess and Stringer published the tale in the autumn of 1844 (Guilds 168).

II.

Castle Dismal, the title of the published volume, is subtitled *A Bachelor's Christmas*, which suggests several contexts for the work. One, of course, is the author's intimate knowledge of the South and his desire, and ability, to bring that knowledge to light and life. Simms's dedication of *Castle Dismal* notes that the story is "illustrative of the traditions of the Southern States" (iii), and the narrator begins his tale with sentimental praise for "the song and the dance, the frolic and the festival" of Christmas in South Carolina (10). Images of the "fatted turkey, the selected ham, mince pies, and the unfailing egg-noggin" lure the reader into what might be a colourful, if superficial, paean to southern customs and the coming together of an entire household around a single table at the holidays (10).

Yet these festivities are not what "The Bachelor's Christmas" is all about. Nor is the tale properly placed in the tradition of "bachelor fiction," though aspects of that genre are also evident. A familiar theme in nineteenth century writing, a protagonist or narrator identified as a bachelor frequented periodicals prior to the publication of *Castle Dismal*. A brief listing of titles appearing in the *Southern Literary Messenger* alone would include "The Bachelor's Death-Bed," "Dorcas Lindsay: or, the Bachelor's Writing Desk," "A Stray Leaf from a Bachelor's Notebook," "The Bachelor Beset: or the Rival Candidates," and "Bachelor Philosophy." These stories, as well as longer works, exemplified the growing uncertainty over the place of the bachelor in a society dominated by ideologies of domesticity.[1]

Ned Clifton, the story's protagonist, describes himself as a "veteran bachelor" (10), and his "terror of the sex" (20) stems from a fear that marriage "destroys many a good heart and generous spirit," turning man into a "tame cur" (12). Clifton is modeled on Benedick, Shakespeare's misogynistic bachelor in *Much Ado About Nothing*, who eventually admits to his love for Beatrice once he is tricked into thinking that she loves him. In the story, Clifton and Elizabeth Singleton do eventually confess their love for each other, freeing Clifton, in his words, from the "melancholy dependencies of bachelorism" (11).

Nor is *Castle Dismal* much of a Christmas story. The joys of this particular Christmas prove illusory. The charm and mirth of the season provide a recognizable backdrop against which Simms can in fact subvert domestic expectations through the unnatural — a bachelor living in the home of married friends, the appearance of ghosts, and an inner story of infidelity and murder that has been hidden by previous generations of inhabitants. The association of Christmas and ghost stories grew through both print and popular custom during the 1830s, although "Castle Dismal" predates Charles Dickens's use of the supernatural to restore the spirit of reunion and joy in such works as *A Christmas Carol*. For Simms, the Christmas ghost story instead casts a heavy gloom over modern, nineteenth-century notions of the home as a haven from a heartless outside world.[2]

Though each of these themes is clearly evident, the most significant context for understanding *Castle Dismal* is found elsewhere. Horace Walpole's *The Castle of Otranto*, first published on Christmas Eve 1764, introduced a new literary genre that came to be called Gothic. Walpole established terror as the dominant element, with its source not only in the presence of ghosts, prophecies, and plot twists, but also in the conflict over lineage and succession. The irrepressible threat that, through the supernatural intervention of God or fate, long-buried secrets of the past will come to light, drives the plot forward in *The Castle of Otranto* and most other Gothic texts. Often this instigating force is the result of some crime committed in the distant past, which must be avenged in order to achieve justice. The transgressor's fears about the disruption of patriarchy and domestic order allow the author to explore extremes of anxiety, cruelty, and passion before the crime is ultimately punished and contemporary conventions of morality are restored (Bleiler vii-xviii).

Walpole exerted considerable influence on the direction of Gothic literature. On the most basic level, the word "Castle" became part of the title for hundreds of novels over the next century, each time suggesting a labyrinthine architecture that complemented the imprisonment of the structure's inhabitants within a claustrophobic world of futility and despair. Themes of terror and horror, guilt and innocence, oppression and persecution were further elaborated in the works of Ann Radcliffe and Matthew "Monk" Lewis. Chiaroscuro became a recurring and almost predictable technique in such Gothic works. Nineteenth-century authors brought an increased amount of supernaturalism, the replacement of ancient castles with more familiar domestic settings, and a greater focus on psychological complexity (Bleiler xiii-xvii).

In the United States, some of these themes could be found in the early work of James Fenimore Cooper, Washington Irving, and Nathaniel Hawthorne, as well as in one of Simms's early novels, *Martin Faber*. The most accomplished American writer of supernatural tales was, of course, Edgar Allan Poe, who emerged in the forefront of Gothic literature in the 1830s with such tales as "Ligeia" and "The Fall of the House of Usher." Poe demonstrated a remarkable ability to unify the elements of character, setting, and mood in the short story to achieve a disturbing portrayal of the neurotic, Gothic mindset (Savoy 181). Thus, the beginnings of Gothic literature in America, according to the literary critic Allan Lloyd-Smith, exhibited a "preference for a more domestic unease and a psychological Gothic, with close relation to the uncanny and the ghost story" (94).

Yet despite evidence that Simms recognized the extent to which he was working within the wider body of Gothic literature, it remains difficult to say what specifically led Simms to choose *Castle Dismal* for a title and the name of the house where the ghostly plot unfolds. Simms may have been aware of a "Castle Dismal" in Robert Bisset's novel *Douglas; or the Highlander* (1800), or he may have been simply continuing the Gothic themes begun by Walpole. Descriptions such as "this dismal old castle" (v. 2: ch. 6) and "these dismal galleries and halls" (v. 4: ch. 18) can be found in Radcliffe's *The Mysteries of Udolpho*. So perhaps it seemed natural to Simms to employ the already well-accumulated discourse of the Gothic in choosing a title. Moreover, Hawthorne gave his boyhood home the appellation of "Castle Dismal" when he returned to it with his wife in the 1840s, although he may have used the name earlier. It seems unlikely that Hawthorne would have taken this name from Simms, since the Salem writer never admired Simms's work. Nor is it likely that Simms would have been aware of Hawthorne's residence. It is more likely that both were inspired by the same Gothic sources but chose the appellation independently (Bloom 28; Gale 458).

Traditional elements of the Gothic pervade *Castle Dismal*. The advertisement preceding the first chapter states Simms's intent to paint events in the lights and darks of chiaroscuro (v). As the narrator, Ned Clifton, approaches his friend's homestead on a "dark and cloudy day" (14), even the lantern at the end of the closed avenue of trees "tended rather to increase than diminish the tone of gloom and coldness" (18). The exterior of the house is likened to a prison or dungeon, and, although the current inhabitants provide a refreshing contrast of mirth, the ghosts of Mr. and Mrs. Potter demonstrate their own imprisonment "by decided and conflicting passions" (54), such that their reenactment of some past scene must be intended in order that the narrator carries out his duty of bringing them to justice in the present. Clifton ominously declares, "I felt sure that what I had seen had been vouchsafed for some special object — that I was to become an agent in some drama of the future, having an immediate connection with some terrible drama of the past" (70-1).

This description of the house and the sensation felt by the narrator upon arriving there are remarkably similar to Poe's setting of the scene in "The Fall of the House of Usher." Though Simms developed his own plot, he retained themes often employed by Poe. The conflicting passions and moral agony of the transgressor or villain, William Potter, and his adulterous wife, would have been familiar to readers of Poe. Ned Clifton reveals even greater complexity in his various moments of interior torment, melancholia, and misogyny. He exclaims that if he had not thought to seek out his boyhood friend, Frank Ashley, for the holidays, "I might have committed suicide, drunkenness, or some other felony" (11). Yet Castle Dismal offers no surcease. The disruption or secret perversion of a place of supposed domestic bliss becomes evident to Clifton, and the relentless heightening of terror grows to encompass not only the suspected, and then confirmed, infidelity and murder that the ghosts re-enact nightly, but also a terror of marriage itself.[3]

In Gothic texts, as in the works of Shakespeare, the characters must either die or marry by the end of the story. For Clifton, the sight of Castle Dismal is not an augury of his own death, but something possibly worse, a dark presentiment "that I might fall into some snares of marriage on this visit." He dismisses this fear "as being quite too dreadful for contemplation" until it becomes apparent that Frank's wife has discovered his "terror of the sex" and determined to match him with one of her friends (19-20). Perhaps it is not surprising, then, that the theme of bringing justice to the ghosts of the haunted chamber is complemented by the story of Ned Clifton's reformation into a soon-to-be-married man.

III.

Critics lavished high praise on *Castle Dismal*. Edgar Allan Poe called it "one of the most original fictions ever penned.... No man of imagination can read this story without admitting instantly the genius of its author" (190). A contemporary critic, Evert A. Duyckinck, a close friend of Simms, deemed it "one of the best ghost stories we have ever read.... We question whether there is anywhere a better manager in the construction of a tale" (1). W. P. Trent, Simms's first biographer, though less inclined to Poe's praise for the story's "supernatural portions," found more appealing "the descriptions of the old homestead from which it took its name" (150). In a 1992 biography, John C. Guilds pronounced the story "excellent" and continued, "in establishing atmosphere, tone, and mood, it is superb" (167). The work was also one of Simms's favorites. He believed it one of the "best specimens of my powers of creating & combining, to say nothing of a certain intensifying egotism, which marks all my writings written in the first person" (*Letters* 2: 224).

The warm critical responses to *Castle Dismal* were matched by strong sales. By mid-January 1845, Simms reported to Lawson, Charleston booksellers had "been compelled to order fresh supplies several times" (*Letters* 2: 13). By June 1845, more than 500 copies had been sold in Charleston (2: 82). The success of the work prompted Simms to propose to Lawson, in November 1845, a second edition. He added, suggestively, "I have an introduction to C. D. Which will improve it, I fancy. It is humorous!!" (2: 113). Soon thereafter a second printing did appear, but with no changes and no introduction. Again, in 1846, Simms suggested to Duyckinck a new, illustrated edition: "its diablerie, illustrated, ... would make a hit" (2: 234). Yet again, in September 1849, Simms urged Putnam to bring out a new edition "from my stereotype plates, to be sent forth with broad margin & fine paper as [a] 50 cent [book], but he never answered me" (2: 557-58). A year later Simms wrote Lawson, "I wish you would get Stringer to put up for me the plates of 'Castle Dismal'" (*Letters* 3: 67). In April 1855, he tried once more, this time with Henry Carey Baird. "Don't you think," he wrote, "that an edition of ... Castle Dismal ... printed on thick paper ... and put in neat colored paper at fifty cents, would be a good speculation? Bad as the book publishing season is, people must buy & read something (3: 382)."

At the same time he was pressing Baird, Simms was preparing *Castle Dismal* for inclusion in a series of "Novellettes" to be published by J. S. Redfield as part of a uniform edition of all of Simms's works that had begun to appear under the Redfield imprint in 1853. Unfortunately for Simms, Redfield temporarily suspended publication during the financial Panic of 1857. As a result, neither

Castle Dismal nor any other title Simms hoped to include in this series of novellas ever appeared, and the Redfield Edition remained incomplete.

In 1863 Simms made one last effort, seeking the assistance of his old friend John Reuben Thompson, editor of the *Southern Literary Messenger*. "Having conceived the idea that a series of my minor tales or novels," including *Castle Dismal*, "would be good selling books, especially now, & for reading in camp and along the highways — (small volumes each of 150 to 200 pages, — & bringing from 50 to 75/100," Simms had sent a proposal to West and Johnson publishers. But they did not respond. Simms asked Thompson to make sure they had received his letter. "If received, their silence is perhaps sufficient answer" (*Letters* 4: 420).

IV.

For some hitherto inexplicable reason, *Castle Dismal* has never been republished since its second issue. How curious. Repeatedly cited as an excellent example of Simms's skills as a story-teller, almost always offered by name to support Simms's claims to a higher literary status than he has generally occupied — yet never republished, even though many of his stories, most of them inferior to *Castle Dismal*, have been reissued, sometimes multiple times.

A recent discovery, described elsewhere, offers tantalizing clues. At various times during the period 1845–1857 Simms worked on what he might have intended to use as the "humorous" introduction to a new edition of *Castle Dismal*. This manuscript fragment, bearing the title "Rawlins' Rookery," tells a story about the writing of *Castle Dismal* and also provides startlingly revealing glimpses into the life and mind of its author. An edition of "Rawlins' Rookery" is currently in preparation for publication, with extensive annotations, and it promises to shed additional light on *Castle Dismal* and its author.

That light will further illuminate the autobiographical elements clearly present in the story. Simms spent the Christmas season 1835, as well as much time after the death of his first wife, at the "Clear Pond" plantation of his friend since boyhood, Charles Rivers Carroll. Carroll's father and Simms's father had both come to Charleston from northern Ireland, and together they became neighbors and members of St. Paul's Episcopal Church. Simms had studied law in Charles Carroll's office and, after the death of Anna and a fire that destroyed Simms's house in Summerville in late 1833, Carroll took Simms and his young daughter Augusta into his household. Thus, for extended periods of time, Simms's address was "Charles R. Carroll, Midway, Barnwell District" (*Letters* 1: xcvii, 68). In 1834 Simms dedicated his romance *Guy Rivers* to Carroll: "true friend, who from boyhood to manhood, has always maintained for me the same countenance — whose friendship no change of situation or circumstance has impaired or affected — whose advice has counselled — whose regards have cheered — whose encouragement, when I would have desponded, has stimulated and strengthened — who would not let me fear, and who taught me a familiar habit of hope — I dedicate this book with a single wish, — not to seem extravagantly selfish, — that it may appear as worthy in the sight of others as he is estimable in mine."

From "Clear Pond," Simms began to court Chevillette Eliza Roach during the winter of 1835-36. After her brother was killed in a duel at South Carolina College, Chevillette was the only remaining child of Nash Roach. A widower, Nash Roach had acquired "Oak Grove," where, styling himself as an English gentleman, he also found himself a neighbor of his first cousin — Charles Carroll. Though Simms may have met Roach and his beautiful daughter previously in Charleston, where both father and daughter sang in the choir of St. Paul's, it was through the aid and mutual friendship of Carroll, and on the grounds of Carroll's plantation, that Simms wooed and won Chevillette (*Letters* 1: lxxvii-lxxviii).

Thus, the courtship story in *Castle Dismal* is remarkably like the Christmas courtship of Simms and Chevillette. Detail after detail in the story reveals an intriguing and sometimes humorous connection, as the reader finds out that Ned Clifton and Elizabeth Singleton (not only the surname under which he published the original magazine version of the story but also the maiden name of the mother he never knew) are 30 and 18 years-old respectively (the same ages as Simms and Chevillette that winter); that Clifton discovers that Elizabeth is an only child; and that he wishes to know if the lady is of a good surname, for he would not marry a woman with an ugly one. Perhaps Simms's own reassurance with regard to Chevillette's maiden name — Roach — was the same reassurance offered to Clifton: "I trust she will suffer you to alter it to your liking" (21). Clifton's host and his spouse also bear close resemblance to Carroll and his wife, Sarah Fishburne.

Simms described Chevillette in a letter to Lawson in 1836: "She is young — just 18 — a pale, pleasing girl — very gentle and amiable — with dark eyes & hair, sings sweetly & plays upon piano and guitar." An almost identical description appears in Simms's description of Elizabeth Singleton in *Castle Dismal*. In his letter to Lawson, he goes on to note that, "in marrying the lady to whom I am engaged, I should be at no expense while living in the South, the case would be very materially altered if I wished to carry her with me to the North during the Summer, as my desire and my pursuits alike would render it necessary to do" (*Letters* 1: 90-91)."

After their marriage, in November 1836, Simms and Chevillette moved to "Woodlands," the property across the Edisto River from "Oak Grove," both owned by Nash Roach. He thus could be financially secure as a full-time writer living on a plantation belonging to his father-in-law. This security would tie him to "Woodlands" and make him dependent on his father-in-law, a widower with but one living child.

To what extent Simms may have actually discussed with Mr. Roach or Chevillette his wish to "carry her North during the Summer" will never be known, but what is known is that Chevillette made the journey only twice, once in 1837, when she was six months pregnant, and a second time in 1844. The first visit included travel by stage coach through the mountains of western Massachusetts as well as time in New York City. Chevillette's experience on this arduous itinerary is not known, but according to Simms, "Madame was somewhat fatigued ... but she bore it better than I expected" (*Letters* 1: 102-03). The second involved a long visit with the Lawsons in New York, during which the Simmses seriously pondered a move north (*Letters* 1: 404). Yet the move never occurred, and Chevillette never ventured north again.

One may only surmise how often the topic of removal to the North may have arisen in the Simms household. Less surmise is required to determine why Simms and his family remained in South Carolina. In 1846 Simms confided to his friend James Henry Hammond, "My wife is an invalid — breeding every year — is an only child — her father advanced in life — unwilling that she should leave home even for a week's visit.... To leave my family, when such a relation subsists between us, is not easy" (*Letters* 2: 247).

That same year Simms wrote to Lawson, "I seriously deliberate upon the propriety of transferring myself, family or not, to Philadelphia or New York" (*Letters* 2: 197). Seven years later he confided to his fellow writer George Frederick Holmes, "My true policy is to live in one of our great Northern cities. Yet my wife is an only child; her father is in declining health & years; she cannot leave him, and I cannot separate from her & my children.... I am thus compelled to remain here, in my stable, when I ought to be speeding down the track" (*Letters* 3: 245).

Finally, there is the evidence provided by the manuscript fragment, "Rawlins' Rookery," a story about the writing of *Castle Dismal* and the unsuccessful effort to track down its author, who has disappeared. In the course of a long discussion of the life of the missing author, his closest friend at last reveals the uncomfortable truth that explains the flight:

> Woman ... in her pure state, is the grand necessity of man. She alone can yield the proper sympathy — can surrender herself to a kindred soul.... If truly loving, she can appreciate any intellect, however subtle, however exalted, and minister to any sensibility, however exquisite & tender. In this

craving he has been disappointed. He chose too soon — chose in the blindness of his need — chose from faith rather than knowledge — chose under his impulse, and not with his soul, and chose through the direction of his boyish passions, at a period of life when choice was scarce possible....

We see such mistakes made daily, and need not wonder. They are the easiest of all mistakes which man can make in life.... You simply deceive yourself. You find pleasure while doing so; and would find the same pleasure, to the end of the chapter, if she, having won, were as solicitous to keep as she has been to catch. But there's the rub. This is not always the case. Perhaps seldom. She, too, has her fantasies and raptures. Marriage undeceives both parties. You find each other out. The Fancy is no longer permitted to contend with the sullen experiences of reason, and Indifference, if not loathing, succeeds to love (72-76).

Confined in his own Castle Dismal, from which there was no escape, and trapped in an unfulfilling marriage, just as Ned Clifton had feared would happen to him, Simms could only dream, and occasionally write, of flight. Begun as a "humorous" introduction to a new edition of *Castle Dismal*, "Rawlins' Rookery" became an outlet for Simms. Misfiled in a folder labelled "Drama" in the Charles Carroll Simms Collection at the South Caroliniana Library at the University of South Carolina in Columbia, it has, for more than 150 years, been either overlooked or consciously ignored by scholars working in that rich source. Its discovery may help explain why *Castle Dismal* has never been republished. It surely affords new and valuable insights into both the story and its author.

V.

Castle Dismal, then, may be read as a southern work; as a work of bachelor fiction; as a Christmas story; and as a Gothic tale. But perhaps more than any of these, and especially in light of "Rawlins' Rookery," *Castle Dismal* is an autobiographical statement and, more specifically, a commentary on Simms's own marriage, which embraces and subsumes all other interpretations. The South is not as it seems. Bachelorhood has its benefits, courtship its rituals. Christmas is not always joyous. Horror lurks just beneath the surface. Marriage is a dismal castle. It deceives and eventually imprisons.

And justice, however cruel and slow to work its will, finally prevails. At long last, and after too long a wait, *Castle Dismal* is again available to readers, to whom now is conveyed the pleasure, and the privilege, and also the challenge, of doing not simply the story, but also its author, justice.

Notes

1. See, for example, Howard P. Chudacoff.

2. See Penne L. Restad (75-6) and Tara Stern Moore (82-3).

3. For more on the connection between *Castle Dismal* and other nineteenth-century gothic works, see especially Lloyd-Smith (7, 32-4) and Molly Boyd.

Works Cited

Bleiler, E. F. "Horace Walpole and the Castle of Otranto" Introduction. *The Castle of Otranto*. By Horace Walpole. Mineola, NY: Dover Publications, 2004. i-xviii.

Boyd, Molly. "'The Fall of the House of Usher,' Simms's "Castle Dismal," and *The Scarlet Letter*: Literary Interconnections," *Studies in the Novel* 35.2 (Summer 2003): 231-42.

Chudacoff, Howard P. *The Age of the Bachelor: Creating an American Subulture*. Princeton: Princeton UP, 2000.

Duyckinck, Evert Augustus. Rev. of *Castle Dismal*, by William Gilmore Simms. *New York Morning News* 1.9 (9 Nov. 1844): 1.

"Editorial Bureau." *Magnolia; or, Southern Monthly* 4.5 (May 1842): 312-320

Guilds, John Caldwell. *Simms: A Literary Life*. Fayetteville: The U of Arkansas P, 1992.

Lloyd-Smith, Allan. *American Gothic Fiction: An Introduction*. New York: Continuum International, 2004.

Moore, Tara Stern. *Christmas in Print*. New York: Palgrave Macmillan, 2009.

Poe, Edgar Allan. "Critical Notices." *Broadway Journal* 2.13 (4 Oct. 1845): 190.

Radcliffe, Ann. *The Mysteries of Udolpho*. 1794. *Gutenberg,org*. Project Gutenberg. 28 February 2009. Web. 29 June 2012.

Restad, Penne L. *Christmas in America: A History*. New York: Oxford UP, 1995.

Savoy, Eric. "The Rise of American Gothic." *The Cambridge Companion to Gothic Fiction*. Ed. Jerrold E. Hogle. Cambridge: Cambridge UP, 2002. 167-88.

Simms, William Gilmore. *Castle Dismal; or, The Bachelor's Christmas*. New York: Burgess, Stringer & Co., 1844.

——. *Guy Rivers: A Tale of Georgia*. New York: Harper and Brothers, 1834.

——. *The Letters of William Gilmore Simms*. Ed. Mary C. Simms Oliphant, Alfred Taylor Odell, and T. C. Duncan Eaves. 5 vols. Columbia: U of South Carolina P, 1952-1956.

——. "Personal Memorabilia," Charles Carroll Simms Collection, South Caroliniana Library, University of South Carolina.

——. "Rawlins' Rookery or the House of Eld and Glamour, A Biography, a Budget, and a 'What Not," Charles Carroll Simms Collection, South Caroliniana Library, University of South Carolina.

Trent, William Peterfield. *William Gilmore Simms*. Boston: Houghton, Mifflin, 1892.

CASTLE DISMAL:

OR,

THE BACHELOR'S CHRISTMAS.

A DOMESTIC LEGEND.

BY THE AUTHOR OF "GUY RIVERS," "THE YEMASSEE,"
"RICHARD HURDIS," &C.

"What, can the grave give up its habitant,
  Or have the sheeted dead a power at will,
  To visit us, and claim their wonted guise;
  And from that eager reveller, the worm,
  Regain their fleshly substance?"
                          BARRY CORNWALL.

NEW-YORK:

BURGESS, STRINGER & CO.

1844.

J. R. WINSER, Printer,
29 Ann-street.

TO

RICHARD HENRY WILDE,

OF GEORGIA.

DEAR SIR:

The present is proposed as the first of a series of fanciful and imaginative legends, illustrative of the traditions of the Southern States, to be followed in proper order by its fellows, should the public taste seem to approve of the sample. I trust that the perusal of these volumes will not prove less agreeable to you, than the present inscription of them, with your name, is an act grateful to your sincere friend and admirer.

THE AUTHOR.

Woodland, S. C. May 1, 1844.

ADVERTISEMENT.

The following story, which was originally designed for a magazine article, has grown into a volume. The purpose of the author was to attempt something of that *chiaroscur* in fiction which is productive of such fine effects in painting,—the distribution, in a novel manner, of his lights and shadows, so as to produce results apart from those which naturally grow out of the events, and which are expected to arise from the mere medium through which they are beheld. He is not so sure that he has carried out his design to his own satisfaction, though he has suffered few misgivings on this head, while going through the task. The novelty of the plan, and the train of imaginative speculation into which it seduced him, while writing, will, he is pleased to believe, sustain the reader, in the (perhaps) more arduous business of its perusal. At all events, it may be permitted him to hope that no one will unnecessarily ask why he departed from his first design, and, in the undue expansion of his staple, rendered his fabric too slender to suffer use. He relies somewhat for this forbearance on the greatly increased indulgence of criticism, which, in this era of 'cheap literature,' seems to have found very conclusive reasons for its own silence. It is very certain that the circumstances which have made original productions cheap, if not plentiful, has rendered criticism circumspect, if not dear. Whether this condition of things portends advantage to either party, is a question that will not concern us now—except, possibly, to take advantage of it. With these few words we leave our ghost-story —for such it is, after the old and approved models —to the tender mercies of the reader.

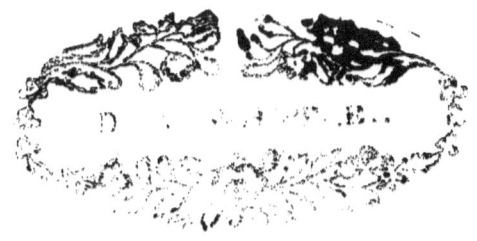

CASTLE DISMAL.

CHAPTER I.

GLIMPSES OF THE DISMAL.

> But how the subject theme may gang,
>   Let time and chance determine ;
> Perhaps it may turn out a sang,
>   Perhaps turn out a sermon.—Burns.

CHRISTMAS was fast approaching, yet I had made no provision for the holidays. I had not as yet succeeded in arranging the plan for the winter campaign. The city was getting monstrous dull. Everybody that could leave it had already taken to himself wings and gone. I, alone, like

> " The last rose of summer,"

—happy summer that leaves such roses —stood solitary in the deserted highways, looking about for my comrades. Something must be done, and right speedily. To delay much longer in resolving—to linger but a single week beyond the next —would, I was very sure—not to indulge in too broad an Hibernicism—have carried me off. And yet, where was I to go—where should I

spend my Christmas—that season, cheering and
cheerful in most Christian countries—but, from
immemorial time and custom, peculiarly so in
Carolina. To leave the city, as soon as possible,
after the first frost, was a matter of course in the
South, however difficult it may be for our brethren, north of Mason and Dixon's, to understand it.
" What's this dull town to me ?"   But where am
I to go?   " That is the question."   There was,
indeed, no lack of invitations and solicitings.   I
was fortunate in my country friends and cousins.
I had two uncles, five aunts, and more than forty
less intimate relations, scattered about the parish-
es, each in full possession of adequate field and
forest.   The ancient manor houses to which my
charter was free as that of the summer libertine,
the wind, were numerous enough.   Many a warm
hall, I knew, would be thrown open with smiles
at my approach, and many a friendly hand would
be extended, with frank and hearty welcome, to
the grasp of mine.   The old haunts, already well
known and gratefully remembered, were still free
to my wandering footsteps ; and the dear, friendly and familiar faces, would rejoice, I was very
sure, once more to encounter mine.   Still, with
all these prospects and convictions, I remained
undecided.   A bachelor is naturally a fastidious
animal, and grows more and more fastidious as
he grows older.   His folly lies in his fastidious-
ness, and cuts him off, no doubt, from many a
pleasant privilege.   He fancies that it confers

others, which, if he himself is to be believed, have
a much more grateful relish. But if there be a
doubt on this head, there is one privilege which
he possesses, the value of which is beyond all question. He has still the privilege of a choice, and
that is something. This privilege was mine, and
the desire to make the most of it, produced in my
mind a degree of indecision which was new to
my habits, and which perfectly appalled me while
it lasted. I turned over the long list of my friends
and relations in positive dismay. I felt very
much like the young devotee of learning, who
finds himself, for the first time, in the midst of a
glorious collection. He is permitted to carry
away with him only a single volume—but which!
I read, and re-read my catalogue. There was
Uncle John and Aunt Mary—there was first
Cousin Ben, and second Cousin Sally—Josey's,
Dick's, Ned's, and Billy's in profusion. One was
famous for his hounds and horses, another for his
wines; a third for his musical and social resources; a fourth for his wit and eloquence;—and
each of these could present his other, and, in some
instances, his most formidable claims, through the
medium of laughing wife or lovely cousin—pretty
sister, who was all fun and frolic, or niece that
could take the field against Taglioni, in a Virginia
reel at least, and sing a song with Mrs. Wood,
Grisi, or Castellane. My aunts, too, were a host
in themselves, not to speak of what they could
furnish. Christmas in Carolina—no longer what

1*

it has been—still brings with it the song and the
dance, the frolic and the festival—the young are
brought together, and the old grow young in the
contemplation of their sports. It was something
more than a fastidious difficulty of choice that
kept me, at the present time, from an easy decision. I felt sure that in whatever direction I
should turn my steps, there would be singing and
dancing, and lots of company, as certainly as the
usual creature comforts—the fatted turkey, the
selected ham, mince pies, and the unfailing egg-
noggin. But I now craved novelty—change—
change. I suffered from that restless yearning
after the unknown, which it may be permitted to
one so remorseless as a veteran bachelor, to experience beyond any of his neighbors. No doubt,
I should find pleasure enough, in any one of the
old haunts—but, with a yawn—"they *are* old, and
I have been there so often already." This weari-
ness of the known is the curse of the vagabondism
which it nevertheless provokes; and I had been
so long and so systematically a wanderer, that it
seemed absolutely necessary that I should still
find out new paths for my restless and impatient
feet. If I did not, I fancied myself growing old
apace, and I could only lose the sense of approaching years, by the constant contemplation
of what was new. New scenes and circumstances, if not new faces, were necessary to stim-
ulate the appetite—already more than half palled
at life's banquet—of a profligate and wasted
youth.

Sitting by my fire, stirring the embers with my poker, and moodily revolving the melancholy dependencies of bachelorism, I suddenly remembered, to my great delight, an excellent fellow—a choice blade after my own heart in youth—who had been my class-mate in college, and who, in addition to other qualifications scarcely less important than the rest, could assert this, that I had not seen him for many years. His lineaments, when I endeavored to recal them, were indistinct in memory ; and an effort to deepen their impression, led me to fancy that I should pass my Christmas with Frank Ashley, quite as pleasantly as with any body else. How fortunate to think of him just at this moment. Had it not been for this lucky suggestion, I might have committed suicide, drunkenness, or some other felony, *a-la-mode Anglaise,* that very melancholy night. Frank Ashley was such a good,—such a glorious fellow,—that is, before he was married—that the very thought of him revived me. Marriage, however, has sometimes a very detrimental effect on this sort of character. But I did not suffer any misgivings to impair the charm of my sudden determination. I thought over all the good qualities of my ancient school-fellow. A thousand petty pranks of our mutual boyhood rose vividly to my recollection. I remembered his love of quiz, of merriment, of a broad practical joke—his hearty enjoyment of all life's pleasures, and the perfect good nature which still predominated even over

the excess of his animal vivacity.—" Where be,"
I asked soliloquizingly, (thinking of Yorick and
Frank together, by a most natural association, and
quoting Hamlet,) "where be your jibes now?—
your gambols—your songs—your flashes of merriment—that were wont to set the table on a
roar ?"

Poor fellow ! I answered these questions with
a sigh from the bottom of my heart, as I recalled
the last communication which I had from him—a
communication inviting me to his marriage—and
which—strange perversity of our nature—he had
actually written in his old terms of life and merriment.   I have read of people who had their jokes
at the gallows foot, and under the axe,—but there
seems to be something very unnatural in joking
about one's own marriage.   At least, such an
opinion may be permitted to one who has a vow
in Heaven against the commission of any such
act in his own person.   Frank's marriage had done
more toward separating us than anything beside.
It destroys many a good heart and generous spirit.
By the last advices—of, not from him—I learned
that he was no longer the same man.   That he
had left off joking and merriment—had settled
down into a plain country farmer; and had been
as completely domesticated in the course of six
months, as if he had been a tame cur of the thres-
hold from the beginning.   " Quite chap-fallen—
to such base uses may we come at last."   My
accounts represented him as good natured and

generous as ever, at heart, but too submissive to betray, in his wife's presence, the good that was in him.

There was something irresistibly ludicrous—remembering what Frank had been,—in fancying him now, in his new character of Benedick, the married man. How could he subdue himself to this condition? He, so ardent, so impetuous—so much governed by impulse—so rebellious against all rule. The thing was unaccountable. The moral problem was beyond my powers of solution. There was but one way left me.

" I will quarter myself upon him this Christmas. I will fathom the mystery by a personal examination."

Frank Ashley was wealthy—had increased his own fortune by that of his wife—lived, as I learned, in something like style,—was, as I knew of old, generous and hospitable—and " Frank, shall be the man !" was the natural conclusion and exclamation to which I brought my meditations as I dashed the poker among the decaying embers and started to the floor. That very night I wrote him to get his " cakes and ale" in readiness, and by return of mail, at the close of the week, I received his answer, couched in a style that left me not a doubt that, whatever might be the altered condition of my friend in other respects, he still kept a corner of his heart for his ancient comrade as honestly as ever. The whole proceeding had so much the air of novelty, that I began, nothing doubting the tenor of his answer, to make my preparations, soon after my despatch was sent. In a week more, I had shaken the dust of the city from my feet ; taking my departure for the country, through that noble avenue over the Charleston Neck, which, according to the celebrated John Archdale, "is so delightful a road, and walk of a great breadth, so pleasantly green, that I believe no prince of Europe, by all their art, can make so pleasant a sight."

But the pleasantness of this sight was soon lost to my contemplations. The day was dark and cloudy, and a few hours after leaving the city it came on to rain, and continued, with moderate perseverance, to rain all day. It was dusk when we came in sight of my friend's domain. It was one of considerable extent. The woods were thick, the population of the country excessively thin, even for Carolina ; the certain consequence of the immense territorial property which was maintained in single hands. The loneliness of the country, with the rawness and cold of the day, tended to make me dull and gloomy, and my approach to my friend's residence did not lessen the gravity of my impressions. The avenue through which we were required to pass in approaching it, was scarcely less than three miles in length. It was one of the closest lanes in the country, only wide enough for a single vehicle, and distinguished by a constant succession of curves that left, at no time, more than

thirty or forty yards of continuous road in sight.
At another time, and under other circumstances,
I should, perhaps, have considered it a beautiful
avenue, but signs are apt to fail in wet weather
as well as dry, and in a cold foggy day in December, an open road is decidedly preferable to
a close one. We like to see the sky on such
occasions, though perhaps there be no sun visible.
Where we rode, neither sky nor sun could be
seen. A passing skirt of cloud, alone, made its
appearance through some little opening which
the trees over-head vouchsafed us, and this
glimpse was just enough to increase the deepen-
ing effect of the gloom into which, a moment
after, the horses carried us. The aged trees,
carefully protected from the axe, from immemorial time, had matted themselves together across
the avenue, and formed an arch-way that was
only not impervious to the rain. That continued
to trickle through, though in its first fall from the
skies it might be heard to beat and patter upon
the branches above, almost as emphatically as
upon the roof of a dwelling. The principal
growth was of oaks, and, grown to monstrous
size, and covered with moss, they stood frowning
on each side of us, like so many bearded giants,
set along the path. Here and there, a tall pine
rose up between, supplying an interval, towering
but slender, like some tall son who has already
overtopped his sire, before he has arrived at
manhood. Vines clambered from one to the

other, and bore in their embrace, as they ran
along from bough to bough, bunches of red and
white roses, the yet undecaying leaves of which
were also strewn thickly along our path. And
this in December. In midsummer, under the
fervent heats of our Southern sun, this avenue
would have been one of the most delicious of all
earthly retreats, but now nothing could be more
gloomy, and I rejoiced with a deep-breathed
sensation of relief, as, emerging from its sombrous
jaws, we found ourselves upon a spacious area,
on which it opened, forming a circular enclosure
of some twenty acres, in the centre of which
stood the mansion.

This building was one of those stern, heavy
looking habitations of the olden time, which our
ancestors appear to have designed rather as pri-
sons than houses. The necessity of a house for
defence, in those days of Indian inroad, was more
obvious than one for comfort. But that antiquity
is altogether comparative, I should be loth to
speak of the dwelling of Frank Ashley as an ancient one ; but in the history of Carolina, it was
decidedly so. It had been a frontier habitation
in the wars with the Yemassees, and had once
been prepared even for an assault from the
French and Spaniards who were reported to be
in the neighborhood, but who did not appear. It
had, at other periods, answered the purposes of a
dungeon as well as a dwelling, and more than
one State prisoner had found secure lodgings for

a night, within its solid walls, while on his way
to trial in the city. The structure was built,
partly of brick and partly of that kind of shell-
work which is called tapia or tabby. We have
old forts of the same material, scattered over
various portions of the South, and still in very
excellent preservation. The brick work had become very dingy and discolored with time and
the weather; but the tapia was almost as fresh
in appearance, as on the day of its first erection.
To the eye of taste nothing could be more dis-
paraging than the gross contrast which was thus
produced in the appearance of the building from
the use of such discordant materials; the whitish
grey of the shell-work mocking completely the
dull, dark, muddy complexion of the brick; but
what was offensive to taste was grateful to antiquity, and the ivy and green moss that clambered
along upon the bricks where they were mouldiest,
served to propitiate the picturesque and reconcile
all minor contradictions. The little clumps of
green lichen that harbored here and there along
the upper walls, stealing upwards even to the
chimney tops, over which, in spite of the smoke,
they hung triumphantly, brought to the mind of
the spectator, the image of some grey warrior of
the middle ages, clad in rusty mail but with a
sprig of holly in his helmet, and a ladies favoɪ
pinned to his breast. The house consisted of two
stories, upon a basement. It was in the form of
a double house, having a grand passage through

the centre, into which the rooms on each hand opened. The windows were few and small. On the eastern side of the dwelling, were the various offices, the kitchen, &c., glimpses of which were indistinctly apparent as we rode into the area. To the North stood a deep, solemn grove, like that which led us to the dwelling, the trees of which, more various than those which composed the avenue, were also, if possible, more majestic and venerable. But a single tree stood in front of the dwelling, but this was the magnolia, that triumph of the woods, with its leaf of brightest green, glossy and glittering, and its flowers of white, that flung an oppressive and powerful odor abroad upon the atmosphere. A lightwood fire, built upon a mound, forming the usual picturesque lantern about the grounds of a Southern country house, shed a strong but flickering light upon the foreground, but tended rather to increase than diminish the tone of gloom and coldness which, at the first moment of approach, the appearance of the whole settlement had cast upon my mind.

First impressions are not often just ones ; and, as a general rule, I have always striven to reject and disregard their suggestions; but, in the present instance, I made the effort without success. The great size of the building—the sombre material of which it was made—its superior bulk and height, so unusual and, seemingly, so unnecessary in our country and pacific times—the extreme age and ghostly aspect of the trees by which it was surrounded—the wretched weather, cold and raw, in which I had travelled throughout the day, and the sunless dusk in which I arrived, at its close—all conspired to maintain in my mind that feeling of solemnity, akin to awe, which had accompanied me almost from the start that morning. I was not the man to form or to believe in presentiments, or my sensations would certainly have produced them. I did, indeed, at one moment apprehend that I might fall into some snares of marriage on this visit,—for a Southern Christmas is apt to produce such disasters in the best regulated families ; but I dismissed this suggestion with some rapidity from my thoughts as being quite too dreadful for contemplation.

CHAPTER II.

THE warm and friendly reception which met me on my arrival, did something towards the dissipation of my gloomy thoughts. Frank Ashley, to all appearances, was the same laughing, good natured fellow as before---as mischievous and impulsive in his movements and feelings as he had been at college ; and his wife seemed as merry a little grig, as ever romped with a kitten. She entered into the spirit of her husband, and though I

had never seen her before, she was as frank and
cordial in her manner as if she had known me a
thousand years.

"And I have known you a thousand years," she
said playfully—" for Frank has told me about the
pranks you have played together.   Ah, Mr. Clifton, by his account, you've been a pair of very
wicked wags in your day."

"Your husband must answer for himself, Mrs.
Ashley, and not for his neighbors.   If mine are to
be believed, no one stands in more danger of being
adopted as the tutelar saint of some holy house
than myself.   I had always a persuasion that I
should one day be an anchorite."

"Ho! ho! ho!" laughed Ashley aloud. "Hear
him, Bess—hear him,—the greatest reprobate for
a school-boy that ever robbed an orchard.   There
is not a melon field in all Saint Philips, that will
not rise in judgment against him."

"I suppose, Mr. Clifton, it is these particular
feelings of yours that have kept you from getting
married?   Celibacy, I believe, is thought to be necessary in religious houses."

The lady asked me this question with an affected demureness that immediately apprised me of
her husband's breach of faith.   He had betrayed
to her my terror of the sex—except at a certain
distance.

"Ah, Mrs. Ashley, I perceive that you know
my weakness.   Your husband is a traitor, after
all."

"No,---on my life;" said Frank. "She has only guessed it. I never said a word on the subject, except that you were unmarried, and, I thought, likely to remain so."

"But we shall see to that, Mr. Clifton, for I give you warning: I have a design upon you. I look for other guests, and to-morrow will bring them. One of these is a lady, of the most wit, of the most beauty, the most accomplishments, the most wealth and worth of any in the District, so——"

"*Gardez vous*, my boy, for you may see that Bess is in earnest. Her very finger speaks."

"And who is the lady, Mrs. Ashley?" I demanded with some curiosity.

"You shall know no more at present. I have said enough to prepare you, and Frank enough to put you on your guard; so that we may hope for fair play at the future meeting."

"Has she any sisters---for I never could think of a woman with sisters."

She is an only child."

"Has she a pretty name? I would not marry a woman with an ugly one."

"I trust that she will suffer you to alter it to your liking."

"I defy you, and all your works," was my playful answer. "My faith is too firmly fixed. I am proof against temptation."

"Well,---be it so, though I trust not, Ned. One thing at least is promised us, Bess. We may at least hope, that the meeting of the parties will bring a merry Christmas to Castle Dismal."

"Castle Dismal! Is that the name of your place?" I cried, catching at the words with some eagerness.

"It is a nickname that Mr. Ashley has put upon it;" replied the wife, with some show of discontent; "the true name is 'Eagle Ærie,' or 'Eagle-Eron.' It has been called by both names, but Frank says that the one is too ambitious and the other involves a contradiction. What do you think, Mr. Clifton;—don't you agree with me that 'Eagle-Eron' should be the name?"

"Milk and mustard! Why, Bess, how can you insist upon such a compound? The idea of an eagle in a cottage! When was such a thing ever heard of before? Besides, ours is no cottage, and lacks all the usual essentials of one. The old name was 'Eagle Ærie,' if either, but is quite too towering for our humble selves, and quiet times."

"But, I beg, Frank, that you will let Mr. Clifton answer for himself."

"Oh, certainly—he may."

"Then, Mrs. Ashley, if I am to be consulted, I most ungallantly decide against you, and with your husband. I am for Castle Dismal, before all—I think that name the most appropriate."

"There!" said Frank, "are you satisfied?"

"No! and, Mr. Clifton, I'd like to know why you think it so appropriate?"

"There's a puzzler!" exclaimed Frank, "you've touched the *amour propre* of Madame, and you'll repent your rashness before all's over. Don't you know that Castle Dismal, or ' Eagle Ærie,' is an old family place of the lady, and her great grandmama ?"

" Now, Frank ! now !" began the wife.

" Turn upon him, Bess. Make him answer. While *he* stands the fire, I remain unscathed."

" Well, Mr. Clifton, do oblige me with your answer. Do you really see anything dismal about us ?"

" No—not about *you*."

" Oh, you evade. About the place. Does it really appear so very gloomy ? Speak candidly, Mr. Clifton, for I declare, I don't know how to believe Frank, when he says it does ;—all my prejudices of family go with it."

" And I should be sorry to disturb them ——"

" Speak without fear, Ned," said Ashley, encouragingly ;—" Bess is not dangerous now."

" Hush you, and let Mr. Clifton speak. Come, Mr. Clifton."

" Truly, then, as far as my first impressions go, I not only think it gloomy, but singularly so. I have never been so much struck with the solemnity of any place in all my life before."

" Indeed !" exclaimed the wife with consternation, while her husband chuckled.

" Yes, to confess a truth, there was something so melancholy and chilling in the first approach to it, that, but for the smiles which I looked to find within, I should have stayed without, and gone further."

"Aye, and fared worse," said Frank. "But when that young lady comes, the scene will brighten. What you say, nevertheless, is thoroughly true. The place has a gloomy look, though Bess is unwilling to believe it. She has always so much sunshine in her little heart, that she has never need to look for it without."

"Oh, Frank!" exclaimed the now blushing wife, as her eyes returned the uxorious glance of the devoted husband.

"Seeing Castle Dismal at night-fall, Ned, makes it doubly dismal; but your impressions confirm my own. I have always thought it a dismal looking place, and hence the name I put upon it. To-morrow, however, when the sun, and ourselves can venture out, it will look more sociable. It will improve upon acquaintance."

"I hope so.—I believe so: but the wonder yet to be explained, is, how you should have fixed yourself in such a place. What could have been the inducement. Your lands are poor ——"

"There you mistake, Ned. We have some excellent reclaimed swamp, which yields a bag to the acre, and some very fair '*mulatto*' pine land which does almost as well. But, I did not buy the place. It was one of Bess's first gifts to her husband, and this, with some family considerations, determined me to give the spot a fair trial. I felt that it was a lonesome place, but it did not impress me with unpleasant feelings because it was so. I was rather pleased with it on this account than otherwise. This, to one who knows my lively temper, may appear something strange; but so it is. It does not lessen my cheerfulness or good humor;—does it, Bess? Probably, if I were an ascetic—a *sulky*, bad-tempered fellow, I should shrink from it with horror, and by the same natural laws which enable me to enjoy it, thrust myself upon that society which would be least willing to endure my presence. Here, with a like selfishness, I shake the uncongenial gloom of the place with laughter, as he would annoy the laughing circle with groans and growlings. He vexes the lively and the living, I, the sombre and the dead. I fancy the ghosts regard me as their most mortal enemy."

" What, you have your ghosts, then?"

" Yes, that we have," was the wife's reply, in a somewhat lower tone.

" They must make the dismals more endurable of Castle Dismal."

" They would if we could see them," said the husband, " but they are timid ghosts, and keep to themselves."

" We have a haunted chamber," continued the wife; " which we have entirely surrendered to their use."

" Indeed! But in so large a house, the wonder is that you have not a dozen."

" Yes, 'faith, Ned,—you will scarce believe it, but we have actually surrendered one of the best chambers in the Castle to their exclusive use. A
2

ghost, you are aware, has always been very careful in the choice of his apartment. It is so in this case. Fortunately, we have room to spare, and there was no motive to join issue with the supernaturals for so small a matter."

" And your ghost stories—what are they? What shape does your spectre put on? What is the gender? What is done; and how do you know that you are thus highly distinguished?"

" You are too many for us with your questions. From my own experience, I should suppose the chamber and the house to be as innocent of any such vermin as the theatre or the race-course. I have seen nothing and heard nothing. Bess has heard a whistle at midnight and a hard breathing in the day; but this ends her knowledge; and our residence here has been so short, and my time has been so constantly and pleasantly employed among the living, that I have not cared to trouble the repose, or enquire into the habits of the dead. The servants, however, are brimful of their marvels, to none of which have I paid much attention, for the simple reason that they are so very silly. They are just such marvels as may be found in any old house of which the rats have had long possession, and now claim by that right. I have heard something more reasonable and sane from the lips of one of our poor neighbors, who once took shelter here from a thunderstorm, and was made to take to his heels by some strange noises which he heard about him; but the fellow was very superstitious, and had previously been possessed on the subject of the haunted chamber, of which he could believe anything. One thing, however, may be admitted certainly, though without lessening our scepticism a jot, and that is, that no one has ever slept in that chamber, to our knowledge, without having been subjected to some alarm or annoyance. My own notion is that the rats are at the bottom of all."

"Then yours is in no danger, old as it is, of being considered a falling house." My allusion was to the old proverb. "But Frank, you have yourself tried this chamber?"

There was a little hesitancy in his reply

"To confess a truth, I have not. Bess is to blame. I would have done so, but she objected for two reasons—the one was that she wouldn't sleep there with me—"

"Well—the other. The first is scarce conclusive."

"The other was that she couldn't sleep anywhere else without me."

"Oh, Mrs. Ashley! you have unmanned the boldest boy that ever robbed an orchard, worried the old wives' tabbies, or defied the cat of the pedagogue! Why, my dear madam, your husband should have won his spurs in that chamber, before you should have said 'yes,' to his fondest question."

"You may win yours tnere, if you are so very

bold; and until you do, I shall persuade Elizabeth Singleton—"

"Elizabeth Singleton, eh!"

"She couldn't have kept it a moment longer
for the world," said the husband; but the wife
continued :—

"Yes, Elizabeth Singleton, and you will find
that all I ever said of her is far less than she
merits. You will think it worth while to win
your spurs in more ways than that if you would
win her favor, for she's as choice as you are, Mr.
Clifton, or she'd have said 'yes' to fifty good
offers or more."

'More or less, Bess ;" said the husband—"fifty
offers now a days is a million to a maiden. But
you don't mean to put off that room upon Ned
Clifton?"

"If he's so very daring, why not?"

"True, why not?" I demanded.

"My husband is a very good husband, Mr.
Clifton," said the lady, "and while he keeps so,
I've no notion of having him carried off by hob-
goblins. Now, you've got no wife to lament
your loss—"

"No children!" continued Frank Ashley, with
an arch smile, which compelled his wife to look
at the wainscoating of the room, while she continued :—

"And if you have no fears for yourself—if you
are as incredulous about ghosts as about wives,
I am clear that you should make the trial of the

Haunted Chamber. We will see how you will win your spurs. I will have it put in trim for you this very night."

"What, Bess!" exclaimed the husband; "expose your guest to a danger from which you restrained your husband? Fie, fie—for shame!"

"And why not, Frank, if he's not afraid? He thinks there's no danger."

"Danger, indeed!" I exclaimed, with a smile: "oblige me, Mrs. Ashley, and have that chamber put in readiness,—not only this night, but every night while I remain with you. Make it snug, give me warm blankets, and a rousing fire, and I'll engage to maintain my hold against all the ghosts in the district."

"Strange to say, Ned," said Frank, "that was the only room in the house that had any furniture when I came first to look over the premises."

"A good reason why the ghosts should give it a preference so decided. Remember, Mrs. Ashley, I make it a point to sleep in that chamber. Only have it snug. These poor pinelands of yours must yield a plentiful supply of lightwood,—let me have enough of it, that I may have a good view of the spectres. I trust your bedstead is strong enough to bear the weight of a tall man struggling with the nightmare. A moderate supper and a tolerably clear conscience, must do the rest."

"But you mustn't forget to say your prayers," said the wife, with becoming gravity. "Now, that is an omission of which Frank is frequently guilty."

" Oh, fie, Frank! Is it possible," I exclaimed, with a look of affected astonishment. " Ah, madam, he was never so forgetful before marriage. No wonder you wouldn't suffer him to sleep in that chamber. You were quite right. I, too, should lack the necessary justification if I were guilty of such an omission."

" I believe you're laughing at me, all the while," she said, good humoredly ; " but we'll see who'll laugh to-morrow. I warn you, Mr. Clifton, if anything turns up to make you feel ridiculous, Frank Ashley is just the person to tell it all to Elizabeth Singleton."

" Ah !" said I, with a sigh,—" you must keep me safe from the living, and I fear none of the hauntings of the dead."

" Really !" said the lady,—" you mustn't flatter yourself that Elizabeth Singleton is the woman to haunt you. She comes here to-morrow, under the belief that we are to have nobody but herself. She is a bookish woman, I tell you. Writes very prettily, talks well, and sings and dances, so Frank says himself,—as if she united a muse and a grace in her own person."

" Why, she is a paragon. She must have had ghostly teachers."

" She is no ghost, however, Ned," said the husband—" but a woman among a thousand. Bess rather warms too much with her subject. She

is a little of an enthusiast in these things—her
house, her husband, and her friend. You are required to believe in Castle Dismal, in Frank Ashley, and Elizabeth Singleton. Of the first, we
have already said more than needful,—of the
second, you perhaps know quite as much, if not
more, than she does herself; and, of the third, I
content myself with saying that she will prove
just about as dangerous an assailant as your
bachelor heart ever had to encounter. She is, in
truth, a very lovely creature. But, as you are to
encounter the ghosts first, we must prepare your
fleshly tabernacle with the needful succor. Our
Major Domo has already made his bow, and sig-
nals the supper table. Will you give your arm
to Mrs. Ashley?"

CHAPTER III.

THE HAUNTED CHAMBER.

THE *salle a manger* was a spacious apartment
in the basement story of the house, and my friend,
with an antique taste, had so arranged its furniture and decorations as to give it somewhat the
appearance of a previous age. The furniture
was massive, of a dark mahogany—pictures of
the chase, of dogs, horses and dead game covered the walls; while, over the mantel, a pair of

gigantic antlers, were so disposed, as to permit of the introduction of a brass socket in the larger portion of each, which received a lighted candle. There was a long slab or sideboard of solid marble, which stood, after the fashion of the old school, forever covered with liquors of the usual kinds. Guns crossed, were suspended against the wall at the head of the apartment, the hooks which sustained them being antlers of bucks which they might have been employed to slay. Amongst these motley exhibitions were two or three dark stained portraits, remote ancestors of my hostess, in whose features I thought I could distinguish sufficient proofs of identity with hers. The table was covered with solid dishes chiefly, with a slight sprinkling of showy ones. Frank Ashley had the fancy of doing things as they did of old. He was proud of being descended of one of the short-lived nobility of Carolina,—a courtly, ostentatious old gentleman, who thought more of the Indian title of Cassique, which he bore, than of any fortune. As he had maintained a sort of state in his household, my friend's vanity,—which was innocent enough,—was pleased to continue it.

"These are holiday times, and we must look for visiters of all classes. The Christmas log must be burning when they come, and Christmas cheer must smoke upon the table. There must be mince pies, of course; and for the drink, Ned, see you yon pile of eggs! We'll have a noggin, to night, or I'm no sinner. How handsomely they did these things in old times, Ned. What state they kept. True, it was ostentatious. What then? It fed the poor,—it filled the hungry. It encouraged the humble. It brought men together, even as benefactor and dependant, and they grew glad and parted with all their doubts and difficulties for a season. All that, however vain-glorious may have been the state which the rich man maintained, seems to be far better than the niggardly reserves of modern times, where we have the stiffness but not the parade—the formality without the feast,—or the feast without the fun. Let it be merry Christmas, say I, as of old, not cold Christmas. The bells should ring out, and there should be free laughter from cheerful voices, and there shall be, Ned, as long as I can have it, though it be at Castle Dismal."

I soon discovered that Frank Ashley had suffered no serious,—no unfriendly change,—in consequence of his marriage. His wife, though she had made his conquest, had yet failed to conquer him. He was a hearty mad-cap still. We sat down to supper, which was no petty exhibition of 'cold baked meats.' These were there of course, but we had a course of fresh fish and warm game beside, and such a display of bread and breadstuffs, as proved the domestic resources of the plantation to be of the most ample description. Let those, however, who delight in voluminous description of the creature comforts, fancy the profusion which was spread before me. As I

2*

confine myself generally to a single meat dish,
and eat sparingly of that, I take no pleasure in
making these details ; and was far more satisfied
when the meal was discussed, and we were again
clustered about the fire-place in the sitting room.
There, after Mrs. Ashley retired, did Frank and
myself sit up, unconscious of the time, renewing
old memories and supplying those gaps in our
several histories of which we were equally ignorant. The evening passed away in the pleasant-
est chit-chat. If there was no wisdom, there was
no absolute folly in the talk, and our mirth, which
was free, was at least innocent. The stroke of
eleven from the clock, warned us that we had
considerably trespassed upon the hours which
the sedate habits of country life had assigned to
the dominions of repose,and my friend announced
himself in readiness at any moment to conduct me
to the haunted chamber.

The room in question was a spacious and com-
fortable one enough. A blazing fire in the chimney gave it an air of life and animation which
must no doubt have been very distressing to the
ghosts for the time it lasted. My good hostess
had preceded us, and had done her utmost to
make it sociable and snug. A small carpet had
been freshly spread upon the floor ; curtains of a
very pretty flowered calico were tastefully arranged against the windows, while others of saint-
ly white descended about the bed. The toilet
was also covered with new garments of white

dimity, from the edges of which, in voluminous folds, depended a deep fringe of cotton, such as is common enough still, to the tidy country households of the old school; and when I enumerate, as in their proper places, the several articles ot chamber furniture, the toilet-glass, wash stand, basin, and all the wonted appurtenances, I had no reason to complain of the accommodations or the apartment which was allotted me. Nevertheless, in spite of all, there was a vacant something in the chamber—a severity—a gloom—which left an impression of coldness upon my mind. The chamber was, in the first place, disproportionately lofty. It had two small windows in the western, and but one in the northern wall; and, it may be remarked that, to a Southern eye, the apartments of a dwelling which lack a southern exposure, have always, during the winter, a sullen and gloomy appearance, and produce gloomy sensations in the mind. The walls were not plaistered, but lined and ceiled with thick cypress plank, heavily panelled in frame-work, and made to appear heavier still in consequence of the frequent employment of deep mouldings, three or four inches in thickness. The boards, from age, had assumed a dark brownish cast. A door that creaked dismally on its hinges as we entered, conducted to the great passage-way of the dwelling, which ran from north to south. The stair flight descended from this passage-way from top to bottom of the house. The furniture of my apartment, be-

sides what has already been shewn, consisted of
half a dozen chairs and a single table. The table
was of a dark wood which I afterwards discovered to be black walnut, and of very great age. It
was equally heavy and ricketty. The bedstead
was of the same material, equally venerable, but
much more stoutly put together. These two articles, as Frank Ashley had previously informed
me, constituted the only furniture which he found,
at his first coming, in the house. These were,
therefore, assumed to be the legitimate property
of the supernaturals, and I examined them in consequence with some curiosity. The bedstead
was singularly tall, as well as massive, and so
very broad that it would have amply sustained,
and yielded sleeping room enough to half a dozen
moderately-sized men like myself. The matrass,
though of the very largest dimensions of those in
ordinary use, did not suffice entirely to hide the
ends of the broad pine rails which spanned the
space between the ponderous beams on either
side, into the morticed sockets of which they fell.

Our survey lasted but a few minutes. Frank
would still have had me change my quarters for
another less questionable apartment.

"You see, Ned, that Madame has done all that
she could towards making you tolerably comfort-
able. But, in spite of all, it looks monstrous cheerless."

"Pshaw, man;" I replied, "would you give
better accommodations to the ghost?"

"No!—but to the living."

"Do not doubt that the living is perfectly well satisfied. Things are as they should be. I don't think I shall take cold here. The room seems snug in every quarter. There are no *panes* out to let *pains* in; and I give myself no concern about the rest. Do you be equally content, and yield yourself to Dan Morpheus with as much complacency as I promise myself to do."

But the good fellow still appeared concerned and dissatisfied with the sombre tone of the apartment, which he seemed to feel even more forcibly than myself.

"I told Bess," he muttered; "to do her best; —and a few more chairs, and a sofa, Ned,— which a servant could bring in a few moments."

"Nonsense, man—your wife has managed every thing with the nice perception of a woman, and you cannot hope to mend it. I am perfectly satisfied."

"Should you wish more covering"—he began, feeling the bed the while.

I threw in an additional brand of lightwood, then, laughing at his anxiety, took him playfully by the shoulder, and shoving him out of the chamber, gave him the "good night," and fastened the door after him.

I was fairly alone in the ghostly chamber, and once more turned about in its examination. To admit a truth, although I had carried it bravely enough in the presence of my friend, yet, when

he was gone, I could not altogether divest myself
of some awkward sensations.   Perhaps, under
the existing circumstances, my disquiet was natural enough; and might have occurred to any
mind just as well as my own.   I was neither more
timid nor more superstitious than any of my
neighbors; indeed, I was generally supposed to
be singularly free from any tendency of this sort
—yet so completely had the haunted chamber
been the subject of our conversation throughout
the evening, and so much had I been impressed
by the strangely dark and sombrous aspect of my
friend's homestead on my first approach, that my
imagination had become actively enlisted in the
matter, and had already begun to conjure up con-
ceits and images of one form or of another,
which put all my senses on the *qui vive*,—though
what it was I had to anticipate, I could neither
exactly say or fancy.   It had been the singular
circumstance in the hobgoblin history of the chamber, so far as it had been committed to my ears,
that nobody could tell, or had told by whom, or
in what manner, it was haunted; and in my more
rational moments, I naturally accounted for the
discreditable reputation under which the dwelling
suffered, by referring it to that impressive aspect
of desolateness, which, from its materials, obscure
situation, venerable woods and antique style of
building, it presented to the eye of the spectator.
So active in its movements, and subtle in its
conjectures, is the imaginative faculty, that, I well

knew, how little aid from the exterior and actual
world it required, to enable it to deal in the most
various and extensive fabrics of self-delusion and
terror, and so long as I could preserve the equi-
librium of thought, this notion maintained itself in
my mind as the solution of all the mystery. But,
having grown weary of my own cogitations, and
feeling myself dowsing rapidly, I said my prayers,
with a laughing recollection of the precautionary
counsel of my more devotional hostess, and laying
myself upon my left side—my usual mode of sig-
nifying to Morpheus that he was at liberty to take
possession,—I went to sleep quietly, without the
slightest fancy that I should suffer any disturbance.
My last thoughts, I well remember, before falling
asleep, related to certain letters which I had forgotten to write before leaving the city—an omission which I proposed to remedy among the first
performances of the following day. Even the
contents of one of the letters, which seemed to
call for more than usual premeditation, were actually conned and adjusted in my mind before I
closed my eyes, and this, too, with as much undi-
verted and concentrative thought, as I had ever,
in my coolest moments, brought to bear upon any
subject. I mention this to show how little my
own mind had to do with the events, wild and
wonderful as they were, which I must leave to
another chapter to describe.

CHAPTER IV.

————— " What may this mean ?—
Visions of terror spare my aching eyes."—ÆSCHYLUS.

I KNOW not, nor can I well conjecture, how long
I slept.   I fancy it must have been several hours.
But I was at length awakened from my slumbers,
which, for the time they lasted, were sound and
satisfactory enough, by a feeling of palsying cold.
My lower limbs were chilled almost to stiffness,
and my first notion on awakening, was, that, while
a more than usually severe change in the weather
had taken place during the night; I had also,
most unseasonably, kicked off some of the most
essential portions of the covering.   But I soon
satisfied myself that such was not the case.   The
blankets and the immense counterpane, which the
providence of my hostess had allotted me, lay upon me still in all the original integrity of their
position.   I must look to some other cause for the
feeling which annoyed me ; and, so little was I disposed to ascribe it to a supernatural source, that I
began to discuss the degree of atmospheric change
that was necessary to produce the feeling under
which I suffered, in spite of the thick clothing which
enveloped me.   It was while thus meditating, sitting half erect in the bed, and groping around with
my fingers, to assure myself of the condition of
the blankets, that I became gradually conscious
of increased facilities of vision.   I found, after a

little while, that I could readily discern and distinguish the remotest objects in the apartment,
which, at my first awakening, had been obscured
in partial darkness. A dim religious vapor, seemed
to diffuse itself throughout the chamber, soft and
soothing, so as to lead me at first to the impression
that the moon was shining through the calico
curtains of the windows. But, it struck me, a
moment after, that the calendar, so far as I could
recollect, had promised us no moon that night.
Next, I thought of comets and shooting stars—
the famous phenomenon of—what year was it?—
being uppermost in my thoughts for a time. This
notion gave way finally to one of fire. I looked
to the chimney place, but there every thing was
black and blank enough. The brands were all
burnt out, and not a spark was visible among the
embers. While I was wondering whence the
light could proceed, my eyes were drawn suddenly to one of the western windows, by an evident
increase of it in that quarter. The reader will
please remember that my bed head stood on the
eastern side of the chamber, close against the
wall, and the fire-place on one side of it, though
at some little distance, to the south. The foot of
the bedstead was consequently to the west. In
the northern wall was a single window, on one
side of which stood the table already described ;
while the wash-stand and the glass above it occupied the space between the two western windows.
The light, still very feeble, seemed to enter through

one of these, and my eyes naturally and suddenly
turned in this direction, from the scrutiny, about
the apartment, in which they had been engaged.
For a few minutes, however, beyond this light or
vapor, I could see nothing—nothing, at all events,
of a more striking or satisfactory character.
There was a degree of uncertainty and vagueness
about my vision which distressed me. I was not
sure that I could grasp the objects which, it seemed to my mind, must be present, and soliciting
my attention. My faculties of sight and thought
seemed mutually confounded. A hazy indis-
tinctness filled the room, which was the more remarkable indeed, as I could see the mere furniture
of the chamber quite as clearly as I should have
done with the ordinary light of a candle; but the
obscurity lay in those portions of the room whence
the light seemed to proceed, leaving me incapable
of beholding, in that quarter, anything save itself.
While I gazed in this direction, I was moved by
observing that the curtains of one of the windows,
were drawn aside—a circumstance which struck
me as not being the case when I retired. While
I was musing this doubt, as composedly as I well
·could—the inquiry was suddenly suspended, and
swallowed up in a newer and more startling occasion of surprise. In the midst of the strange
light, to which, by this time, my eyes had become
a little more reconciled, I distinctly beheld the
outline of a human form, which emerged, as it
were, from behind the curtain. The figure was

slight—so very slight and shadowy, that I had almost come to think it the reflection of one in a
mirror from some other part of the chamber;—
but with my increasing steadiness and improved
vigilance of vision, I was made to think otherwise
a few moments after. In short, I soon knew the
intruder to be a woman!

A woman! Here was a discovery! What had
a woman to do in a bachelor's chamber? I was
beginning to ask myself whether such audacity
did not merit some severe penalties, when I was
startled by a whistle, faint but clear, which sounded from without the apartment. It rose, so I fancied, directly beneath the window; and I was
confirmed in this impression, as the woman, in the
next moment, glided once more behind the half-
opened curtain, as if to peer through the pane.
Here she remained a few seconds, then turning
quickly round, I was enabled, for the first time, to
distinguish, with tolerable clearness, the features
of her face; my capacities for observing them
closely, being impaired only by the singular in-
tenseness with which her eyes appeared to fasten
themselves in a keen scrutiny upon my bed, and
even, as I fancied, upon my own. I could scarce
draw my breath under this strange examination,
and strove not to do so, for fear of losing the opportunity, thus offered me, for surveying to advantage the face and person of the intruder. I could
thus behold every feature with tolerable distinctness. She was in a night dress; her hair, which

was tied at the crown, had escaped, probably from
a cap, and now fell in a single and heavy mass
upon one of her shoulders, the ends of it being
apparent in front of her person. Her complexion
seemed to be singularly fair.   The face was that
of a young woman, certainly not over twenty
years of age, who, in ordinary parlance, would be
pronounced rather pretty than otherwise.   Her
eyes were dark and full of an eager vivacity, which
was not unmixed with anxiety and apprehension.
I may add that her glance, at the same time, was
expressive of other feelings, which spoke neither
for a conscience free from reproach, nor for the
presence, then, of purer desires than those which
had prompted her to previous guilt.   In short, the
glance was salacious, with the anxious incertitude
natural to unappeased desires, and betokened the
activity of passions having all the tendency of sin,
without the audacity which they necessarily ac-
quire from habitual indulgence.   Such a countenance, in the daily walks of town or country,
would be pronounced that of a vain, weak, silly
creature—one who would easily fall the victim of
her own equal feebleness and vanity, under the
adroit management of any practiced profligate.
It may be supposed that my survey was conducted under very conflicting feelings. I had my
doubts and conjectures, not altogether unmingled
with my apprehensions, of all that I witnessed.
Could it be that my friend was mischievously prac-
tising upon me ? Such a joke would have been

precious enough to both of us in the days of our merry and irresponsible boyhood. But then, I knew certainly that he was too well acquainted with the usual firmness of my nerves, to fancy that such an attempt would prove productive of much profitable fun. Nay, the same knowledge which he possessed of my temper, would have naturally led him to apprehend some danger to any agent who might be employed in such a proceeding. If I had any suspicions of him, they were momentary only. Could it be that I was affrighted by a phantom of the sight, or one merely of the brain—the conjuration of a diseased mind, or of an intensely excited fancy? This, the very fairness and deliberation with which I then discussed the matter in my own mind, naturally forbade me to believe. Perhaps—and this conjecture inspired me with very different sensations—perhaps my visitor was some living sinner—what more likely? —who had been accustomed to make this chamber the theatre of her ill-practices, and was sufficiently audacious to continue them, under the supposed salutary dread which the reputation of the apartment was calculated to inspire. As this idea entered my mind, I began to think of starting out of bed and of punishing the offender for her impertinence; but just at that moment, to my great consternation, she resolutely approached the couch where I lay; and, to the discredit of my manhood be it spoken, the effect was a complete surprise upon me. I was perfectly paralysed by the

movement. A cold chill suddenly possessed me.
My limbs were stiffened; my joints seemed utterly nerveless. I felt all the bitter and humiliating
sense of utter incapacity. I could not have raised
an arm in my defence. I could not have lifted a
foot in flight : nay, I felt that my voice would not
have sounded beyond a whisper in the hollow
and cold caverns of my throat. I was struck
with a sudden apathy which made me motionless ;
and yet I could feel the pang of the incapacity.
My powers of thought seemed to be more active
than before. My sense of observation was as keen.
I resolved—I think without dread, and in the very
mockery of fear—to leap upwards and defy the
phantom, whether it were of sight or mind. But
my physical man failed to co-operate with the resolve of my mental and moral nature ; and I lay
cold and passive while she drew nigh, and bending over me, looked down into my very eyes.
Shudderingly and involuntarily, I closed them. I
could not endure more than the first glance of that
intense and glistening eagerness which shone out
from hers. They seemed to look through me—
to pierce me with a sudden pang of cold, like a
frozen arrow ; and to benumb, as with a serpent-
like sublety of poison, the very life-blood and mar-
row of my brain. But, in the momentary view
which was permitted me, my first impressions of
her countenance were all confirmed. There was
all the trembling anxiety of passion—its eagerness, its hope, its fear, its tumultuous intensity.

There was also the stare of guilt—the glassy gaze, as if the worm of conscience were busily gnawing in the same abode where lust ruled openly triumphant. Though passion was there the master, it could be seen that there was still a warfare which it was compelled to carry on with active and opposing emotions. The movements of the phantom, though prompt and quick, were evidently stealthy; and, still apparent—and at moments predominant over their usual expression of salaciousness—I could read in her eyes the dread of detection—the last remaining proof, not of a lingering virtue, but of a wholesome fear of those higher human powers, which had the right, when suffering wrong, to punish it. But all these things and thoughts were of instant duration only. The blood in my veins began again to thaw. In a few moments I felt relieved of that chilling pressure which had " sate so heavy on my soul." Without unclosing my eyes, which I almost feared to do, I felt assured that the obtrusive spectre had withdrawn. The cold departed from my limbs. My blood was now rushing with something like the impetuosity of a mill-sluice which has broken its banks, and coursing down, in joyous freedom, from the citadel whither it had fled for refuge. I looked up, and beheld the faint outlines of the figure, as it glided from the window, through which it seemed to have been gazing. It stopped for a moment before the mirror,—

" Heedful of beauty, the same woman still,"—

and appeared to indulge in that " sly glance or
two," for which, as Anacreon Moore tells us, in
one of his exquisite butterfly ditties, a damsel
" never wants time,"—then glided rapidly towards
the door which stood near the chimney in the
southern wall of the chamber. Here she paused for
a few seconds. Her eyes were again fixed upon
the bed, and, as I fancied, in eager inquiry, upon
myself. The intensity of their expression—the
anxiety and the dread—seemed now to be greatly
increased. There was a look of trepidation and
alarm, almost amounting to terror. But I had not
time for more. In another instant—almost before
I could note in what moment, or how—she disappeared from my sight and from the chamber.

I breathed at last—a breath that was almost a
gasp—so long had my breathing been suspended
in the excited emotions which I felt. I was beginning to shake off my terrors and to recover
my suspended manhood. Already had I begun
to reproach myself with my imbecility—nay, I
was half vexed with myself at my want of gallantry, in not having shewn a proper courtesy to
my fair visiter ;—but my compunctious feelings
on this score were very soon forgotten in a second
occasion for wonder and alarm. My limbs were
suddenly invaded by a second chilling sensation,
and again breathless, and again unnerved I sank
back, gasping, but still gazing, with apprehen-

sive eagerness upon the entrance through which
the damsel had disappeared, and from which I naturally looked for her to re-emerge. But, in that
quarter, I beheld nothing. I next looked to the
window,—but all was vacant there. Still my
cold sensations continued, and while I lay, wondering by what on earth, or in heaven, they could
be occasioned, mine eyes were suddenly drawn
to a point much more alarmingly near than either
door or window. There, at the very foot of my
bed—apparently seated upon it, and perhaps, for
aught I could tell, pulling on his stockings, was
the figure of a man in his night-clothes. His face
was from me and turned towards the entrance.
He seemed actually to have just arisen from the
couch in which I lay so snugly covered up. In
this way, he sat for a space of twenty seconds,
and, in all this time, I watched him deliberately. I
seemed to feel, in this survey, much less constraint
and apprehension than while gazing on the female. It was very remarkable, however, that,
though he was so much nigher to me, all the time
than she, yet I beheld his ·form and features with
far less distinctness than I had done hers. There
was less of that strange mysterious vapor throughout the apartment after her absence. The ordinary objects of the chamber were less apparent.
About him there was a cloudy atmosphere—I
saw him as through a thick, murky veil—just such
an outline as appears to one of himself, in a mirror overspread with mist.

3

At the end of the period mentioned, he rose
from the bed, and for a moment stood erect and
motionless.   Then, with a movement equally
noiseless and deliberate, he glided towards the
window, through the glass of which he appeared
to gaze with much intentness.   Turning about,
finally, I was now permitted to behold, though
still, as in a glass darkly, the features of his countenance.   They were those of a man rather over
forty years of age.   Manly, naturally pleasing and
expressive, they might still, in moments of repose,
be considered attractive.   In youth, they must
have been handsome—were still symmetrical,
free from wrinkles, and delineated with remarkable freedom and fullness.   His complexion was
dark and manly—his form large and somewhat
inclining to corpulency.   His hair, originally
black, seemed to be somewhat freely sprinkled
with the frosts of an early winter.   The *tout ensemble* of his air and features, was that of a man
naturally intelligent, thoughtful, inclining perhaps
to severity; expressive of firmness, much simplicity of character and· great deliberation.   But,
however these might denote the character of the
man in repose, their present expression—his passions being all in action—was of a very different
kind.   Anger, amounting to ferocity, was the prevailing expression—subdued, however,—in one
sense of the word—by an air of the keenest mortification.   His hand, at one instant, was clenched, as if to fell an enemy,—the next moment it

was stuck into his hair, from which it was not withdrawn without tearing out numerous shreds, of which he seemed utterly unconscious. Some moments followed, given, it might be, to stupor,— possibly to reflection. Once more he proceeded to the window, looking out earnestly through the closed sashes,—then returning, he stood awhile in the centre of the chamber, and gazed upon the couch where I lay, with the look of a man who has just surrendered the last and dearest hope in existence. Never was despair more legibly or forcibly written upon any human countenance. But he remained not long in this attitude. A more passionate expression, if not a darker, now overspread his features. Then I beheld him distinctly take from a peg in the wall, a huge cloak, in which he wrapped himself. This excepted, his only other garment was the night dress in which he appeared to have slept. His determination seemed to be made, and, with a somewhat hurried movement, he disappeared, almost as suddenly, through the same door by which the female had departed.

CHAPTER V.

DOUBTS BY DAYLIGHT.

I was thus at length relieved from my annoyances. Man and woman, husband and wife—if

such, indeed, was the tie between them—had
both disappeared. During the presence of the
former, I had not felt the same degree of en-
feebling surprise and apprehension which had
overcome me while the latter lingered in the
room. Perhaps, as it was she who had made
the first demonstrations upon me, her appearance
had reconciled me to his. Familiarity had, in
some little degree, brought with it contempt.
But, in truth, there were other reasons why the
last spectre should be less impressive than the
first. There was in the face of the female a conflict and sway of evil passions which had been
painful to look upon. The expression of countenance in the man, had been, it is true, sufficiently
dark, deliberate and ferocious. But it was more
decidedly human ; and there seemed, in the character of the accompanying circumstances, to be
something of a justifying cause for that bitter
and angry look which his features wore. The
details, so soon as they had both disappeared,
and left me free to reflect and remember, were
such as to shape out to my mind a distinct and
cohesive narrative of cause and effect ; as closely
welded together as that of a law case, well put
by an experienced master of jury pleading, at the
Court of General Sessions. So much did the
affair excite my thoughts, doubts and serious
wonderment, that I hoped for no more sleep that
night. I remained, wakeful and watching,—still
anxiously expecting the reappearance of my noc-

turnal visitants—until broad day-light, when, according to popular faith, such wanderers are required to return to their several prison-houses. I bitterly reproached myself that I had forborne to speak to, or to pursue, them. I accused myself of imbecility in this matter, with a sense of shame which I had not thought it likely I should again feel, and which flushed my cheek with more than one burning blush. I had certainly behaved very much like a school-boy, compelled to go to bed in the dark, in a very suspicious and ill-looking apartment, or to trudge along, with uncertain footsteps, and terror momently increasing, beneath the wall of a church-yard after vespers.

But, with the full blaze of day-light upon me, the question was to be seriously asked of myself, whether I had dreamed or not? There were sundry good reasons to make me fancy that I had. There certainly had been no moon that night. The night had been dismally dark—the skies starless, covered with clouds, and shedding a chilly, drizzling rain throughout the better part of the hours. Whence, then, could that light have been derived, which, seeming to enter at the window, enabled me so clearly to ascertain objects in my apartment, and even to distinguish their features? In the room, itself, there were very cogent reasons to disprove my faith in the spectres of the night. The curtain, which I had seen drawn aside when the woman appeared

looking through the window, remained undrawn
in the morning, and precisely as I had left it on
retiring to bed. The door of the chamber, which
was latched when I rose, precisely as I had
latched it myself, on Frank Ashley's leaving me,
was one of those creaking, croaking old doors of
a venerable mansion house, that, swinging to and
fro, send their complaining groans through every
apartment, and will not suffer themselves to engage in any movements that require secrecy and
silence.

And yet, there were some strong arguments in
favor of my senses also. There was something
very remarkable, and quite beyond the usual
power of dreams, in this singular dependance, of
one upon another, among the several circumstances that had awakened my attention. The
strange distinctness with which I had been permitted to note and to analyze the features of persons whom I had never before beheld—features
so distinguished, too, by decided and conflicting
passions—as well in the face of the man as in that
of the woman ;—and those passions so apparently
due to the very situation of the parties, and that
situation one which would be apt to make itself
felt and understood by minds of the most ordinary
conjecture ! I had such a clear idea of both
faces in my memory,—I had such a perfect conviction of the feelings which seemed to govern,
for the time, both of their hearts,—that I felt it
impossible to divest myself of the certainty and

naturalness of all that I had witnessed. Still what could I say to my host and hostess? To tell them what I fancied myself to have seen, and to tell them nothing more;—to admit that I was so daunted by the visit as to be incapable of acknowledging it by any of the usual courtesies,—unequal, as I was, to the task of speech or motion;—I, who had been so bold the evening before—"so confident against the world (of ghosts) in arms"—was more than my courage and philosophy could think of; and when I heard Frank's knock at my chamber door, at sunrise, I hurriedly resolved to practice a little deception upon him—to confess to nothing but some idle and incoherent dreams, which I neither could, nor cared to, remember;—and to render my story the more plausible, I pretended a most incorrigible fit of sleep which his knocking failed to disturb. He finally aroused me, by entering the chamber, and giving me a hearty shake of the shoulder, which, at length, produced the desired effect.

"Well!" he exclaimed, in anticipation of my premeditated fabrications; "I perceive, from the soundness of your sleep, that you have had little or no annoyance from the ghosts. I knew that you were just the man to stifle that superstition, and to make me richer, by one apartment at least, than I had been before. I consider this a very fair trial of the haunted chamber, and shall have no scruple now to put into it the first pretty little damsel that comes to see us in a crowded time. How did you sleep, Ned?"

It was with some difficulty that I kept down the struggles of conscience, in obedience to the sort of prudence by which I felt disposed to govern myself. I answered, however, with tolerable boldness.

"Surely, Frank, an unnecessary question. You ought to know—nay, for that matter, you can better answer than myself. How did you find me?"

" Sound as the seven sleepers, sure enough."

To help the lie, I rubbed my eyes with exemplary industry, and a yawn of brobdignag dimensions accompanied and enforced every syllable I uttered.

" The room is a good one," I continued—"too good to be given up to the rats, or ghosts, for probably they are one. The prettiest and timidest damsel in the country might sleep in it safely. I trust, for my own part, I may never find a worse."

" And you had no disturbance, whatever?"

" None ! I dreamt, I believe, some ghost stuff during the first part of the night—probably in consequence of our previous conversation ;—but it gave me very little concern at the time— was too stupid to excite, and too incoherent to be remembered."

" Well, hurry on your clothes, and come down to breakfast. We are all waiting, Bess

was quite anxious to know whether you had
survived the night ; and speaks as confidently of
your having been ghost-worried, as if it were the
surest article in her creed. You will have to
make a ghost story to meet her requisitions."

"Tell her how you found me, Frank."

"Ay, ay!—but hurry, hurry."

"I will—make my compliments, and, say that
I shall delay the coffee but a few moments longer."

He left me, and, while completing my toilet, I
nerved myself to the meeting with my pleasant
hostess. It was not very difficult to baffle her
curiosity, though she was rather more suspicious
—more observant and curious, I should say—
than had been her husband. Frank had known
me sufficiently long to believe that I could not
easily be daunted by the supernatural ; and his
own scorn of the idle stories of the ignorant, rendered him easy of access to any assurance which
was calculated to strengthen his previous opinions.
With our united efforts—he innocently contribu-
ting to aid my plan of deception—we contrived to
satisfy my hostess ;—not that her haunted chamber had been slandered,—for she would scarcely
have surrendered her favorite superstition on any
terms,—but that I had succeeded, from sheer
stupidity or recklessness,—in sleeping through
all its ghostly performances. Still, though I had
thus easily got through the opening scene, I had
a part to perform throughout the day, which I
found anything but easy. It would not do for me,

3*

with my reputation for animal spirits and philosophical phlegm, to suffer myself to appear ab-
stracted and thoughtful—to be caught moodily
chewing any cud of thought which might seem to
be furnished by very grave and absorbing in-
fluences.   This would prompt conjecture, and
rouse suspicion, and I was every now and then
warned of what was expected of me, by observing, in spite of all my caution, that the arch,
piercing, inquisitive eyes of Mrs. Ashley were
fixed on mine, with looks of distrust, if not of
downright doubt and suspicion.   My part became momently more and more difficult, as, with
each moment, I really became more and more
thoughtful.   My mind wandered from me at frequent periods—my fancy was continually active
in presenting to my sight the shows and images
which had annoyed me through the night.   They
seemed to crowd upon me on every hand, from
quarters in which I could least apprehend the appearance of such—now gleaming suddenly ath-
wart my vision, as I changed the direction of my
glance,—now looking at me from the cup as I
raised the coffee to my lips.   The sudden address
of my host or hostess, occasionally, seemed to
startle me, and the entrance of an unbidden servant actually caused me to shudder with the ex-
pectation of something to follow in the shape of
my nocturnal visitants.   The face of the woman,
in particular, seemed to meet me at every turning, and, whenever hers would disappear, I could

fancy its place occupied by that of the man. They did not seem so much like images and shadows of the mind, as positive and long known personages—people with whom, at a remote period, I had been well acquainted, and in whose fortunes, by some means or other, I was required to feel an interest equally active and permanent. As the day advanced, my distresses of thought increased;—mentally, I felt more miserable, than I had done during the night. Then, as I have said, my sufferings seemed almost entirely physical, in which my mind took part only because of its mortification at the imbecility of my body. Out of the house as in it, my annoyances increased. I was haunted in every situation by these thick-coming fancies; and so very annoying finally did their hauntings become, that, ere the day was ended, I had almost grown heedless of the necessity, which I had felt so strongly in the morning, of concealing my disquietude, under the shows of an indifference and mirthfulness which at no period did I feel. But something is to be told of my friend's grounds, which I examined during the day—a portion of these grounds, as the sequel will show, being of no small importance to our narrative.

CHAPTER VI.

THE ANCIENT GROVE.

THE appearance of Ashley's plantation, in the daylight, and under the clear but subdued sunshine of a December morning, did not very materially alter those first ·impressions which I had received on beholding it the day before. It was a noble estate, broad fields, numerous acres, a very proper arrangement of grove and meadow, thicket and opening, but still there was a something about it, or a lack of something, which left it cheerless and without attraction to the eye. My friend could point to various objects that in themselves might be considered pleasing and even beautiful. His trees were of the noblest, most majestic fashion; his groves and thickets had felt the forming hand of taste. Art had thrown up its mounds and crowned their heights with statues. There were no fewer than five leaden images that might have been Grecian gods, or Indian chieftains—the skill of the sculptor in adjuncts, not having been such as to render determinate his objects. Artificial ponds were doubly attractive as affording relief to the plain, and trout to the table,—and the flower garden, and kitchen garden, were such as would make smile the severest housekeeper. But these did not suffice to rid the *tout ensemble* of that pervading aspect of antiquity and gloom which had oppressed me from the beginning. The trees were nearly all of them old and massive. It was as if the fathers of the forest had survived their young, and were destined to die childless. The young shoots—what there were—the shrubs and undergrowth—which were to constitute the hopes of succeeding generations— were shrivelled, stunted, and seemed already in possession of the worm. I almost fancied, in the language of Wordsworth,—that, however beautiful it might have been,—

"Something ails it now, the spot is cursed."

Certainly, it seemed as if some doom had suddenly gone over it. The abandonment of the place for several years, during the childhood of its fair mistress, had directly contributed to this effect. The savage practice, rather too general in the South, of burning the woods in order to hasten the growth of the herbage in the cattle-ranges, had kept down the inferior vegetation; and, without a resident, on the spot, to protect it from the fire, that of the neighbors, at every succeeding spring, had crossed the boundaries, and ravaged at pleasure, and without intermission, blazing up to the very doors of the dwelling. The effect of a deficient undergrowth upon trees already old, is peculiarly melancholy. Like old people who have survived their children, they seem never to have been young themselves. Preserved from the axe, while the smaller growth perished by the fire, they grew to enormous size, possessing them-

selves of all the space, their trunks amply proportioned to their immense height, and fully able to
bear the weight of that luxuriant wealth of top,
which, covering all below, stretched out a thousand hands in search of room above. Some of
the woods into which we wandered might have
suited worthily the dark and savage rites of the
ancient Druids. Their limbs and leaves, closely
knit above, formed numerous and well arched
passages below, into which the sunbeams never
darted, or in partial and trembling effusions only ;
like so many shy and timorous spirits, for ever apprehensive of detection. It does not need, however, that I should dwell on these appearances.
It is quite enough to intimate the causes that ope-
rated to give strength to the superstitious feelings
already active in my fancies. I certainly felt
myself chilled by all I saw, with the exception of
my old friend and his lovely wife ; and it was
only wonderful to me how one so merry in his
boyhood, and with an appetite, in his youth, forever on the wing after mirth and pleasurable excitement, should be so well content to consume
the better hours of his manhood in so dreary an
abode. I could not forbear the expression of my
surprise on this subject.

" Somehow, Frank, my first impressions are all
confirmed and strengthened. The aspect of your
place, in the sunshine, fails to soothe me. It sub-
dues—it awes me. It is something unnatural to
behold antiquity on the face of our country. I

certainly did not expect to find it here.   There is
a lowering, dark, mysterious something about
your grounds, your house, your groves, your
gardens, even——"

" In short!" he exclaimed, playfully interrupt-
ing me—" about everything that is mine."

" No! no! By no means.   You are, to all appearances, pretty much the same ; and I give you
due credit for the excellence of your choice in a
wife.   She, it seems to me, is the very picture of
good humor."

" The very reality, you should say."

" I believe it;—but, truly, there is about the
place a certain air of desolateness——"

" In spite of me, my wife, and my white pal-
ings ?"

" In spite of all, and my own wishes to behold
all that is yours through the most rose-colored
medium."

" Poh, poh, poh!   You have a fit of the blues,
Ned,—nothing more.   You see as through a glass
darkly.   The third morning hence, you will
awaken, and fancy it the loveliest spot in the District—in any District.   But that will be in spite
of the solemnity, and perhaps, because of it ; for,
I confess, there is something sad and gloomy in
its appearance ;—not cold and desolate as you are
pleased to phrase it ; but this rather commends
it to my taste than not.   Born-laugher as I was,
Ned, I still confess to a passion for the peaceful—
for what is quiet;—and he who really loves the

quiet and the peaceful, will not object to it because
it sometimes appears to his vision, caparisoned in
the garments of the solemn and the sad. Talk-
ing of the solemn, reminds me of a spot which I
have not yet shown you. Turn with me into
this grove. This is a place to increase your
gloom. In such a spot as this, one might fancy a
grave for himself and his friend. See these trees!
What gigantic sovereigns do they seem! They
so completely shut out the sun, that there is no
undergrowth; and their leaves of perishing yellow, how they carpet the spot! Now, as you
walk among them, you feel sad, serious thoughts;
but, surely, not unpleasant ones! Here, I wander
and contemplate; and, sometimes, when the days
are warm and pleasant, Bessy comes out and joins
me here, and we sit down beneath these grey
warriors of the past, and wonder at their histories. Here, you perceive, is a magnolia;—one
of the wonders of our forests. It is more than
one hundred feet in height, and is, perhaps, a thousand years old. Look at the initials cut upon it;
the dates to several suggest ideas of antiquity
even here. 'J. G. 1721.'—That chap, whoever
he was, must have been one of the first settlers
of the District. Here is something that will prove
to you that the spot did not look gloomy and dis-
couraging in other eyes. Here are some love-
tokens. The artist has wrought a pair of hearts
most effectually together, and clenched them with
an arrow. 'W. & E.' below, invite us to ask

questions which neither of them now can answer.
The date—1750—something later, is yet of five
or six generations passed. My employment is to
come here and conjecture what may be the history of these lovers. Did they meet here? Sat
they together on these little hillocks? These old
trees may have heard many a love story—nay,
Ned, may have witnessed many a tender smack,
about which, dumb chroniclers, they can tell no
stories. How you can think the place gloomy,
and feel it cold, is a mystery to me."

But I did not think the spot cold to which he
had drawn my attention. On the contrary, it
seemed to me more genial, more encouraging,—
strange to say,—than any other part of the terri-
tory. To the ordinary eye it would, no doubt,
have seemed the most decidedly solemn of the
whole,—and it was in consequence of this very
decided and unqualified characteristic that it had
less of a solemn influence upon my mind. It
seemed to have been set apart as a place devoted
to sad musings, and for this reason, I did not find
it irksome. It was fitting for its purpose. It was
natural. I was beguiled, too, by the fanciful conjectures of my friend on the subject of the lovers.
What scenes, indeed, might not this grove have
beheld? What scenes of love and tenderness, of
hate and strife! What picturesque adventures
of the lonely red hunter! What wild instances
of conflict between him and his conqueror! Who
had first planted the standard of civilization in

this remote spot when it was the frontier ?—And
what bold dame had first ventured, with her
stronger, but scarce firmer husband, to carry with
her the domestic gods, and set them up here
among these giant oaks and towering sycamores?
The contemplative mind might, indeed, with but
small aid from the imagination, find sufficient employment, and materials enough for the most curious conjecture, which would furnish clues to a
thousand passages of story, no less true, perhaps,
than romantic.   These notions, together with the
protracted examination which we bestowed upon
the spot, necessarily renewed, in my mind, the
impressions which had been made upon it, by the
phantoms of the last night.   Did these phantoms
have any interest or connection with the initials
carved upon the tree?   Were the images which
had startled me from my slumbers, and so effectually banished sleep from my eyelids, those of
the parties, who, in hours of fearlessness and hope,
and perhaps of love that knew not how to doubt
the truth of the beloved one, or to apprehend
either the decay of faith or beauty—in a dreamy
fondness—made these records, rude and gothic as
they were, which had yet survived hundreds, made
at a like period, upon the less enduring marble ?
If they were the same, how strange the similitude
between the appearance of their dead records
upon the still green and flourishing tree, and the
re-appearance of their wan and buried aspects
upon the hours of the yet unburied time !   My

meditations grew momently more abstruse and solemn. A deeper interest enveloped the mystery of the night, as I thus unconsciously strove to couple it with some one of the otherwise unmeaning letters, dates, and symbols, which were numerously cut in the tree before me. But the scene I had witnessed did not speak for love between the parties who were the actors in it; but it told for a foregone conclusion of love, when it implied jealousy and suspicion in one, and conscious wrong and falsehood in the other. But conjectures like these were premature, and I finally dismissed them from my thoughts.

It was certain that, in approbation of my friend's taste, the grove had been a favorite haunt in ages past, for others, who had sensibilities and hopes, and, perhaps, some strong ambitious tendencies. Though in some respects a vanity, it is yet one of an elevated kind, which seeks to make its record before it dies, and to leave an inscription behind it. The ancient possessors of the grove, like my friend, must have been contemplative and thoughtful people, to whom sad images were not unpleasant ones; though, in the instance of a heart so light and joyous as his, I should have been the last to think they could be desirable. As we emerged from beneath the dense umbrage of this venerable wood, at the point opposite to that by which we had entered it, my eyes were involuntarily cast upward, when I beheld the mansion house, unexpectedly, but a

short distance from the spot.   Looking down
directly upon the grove, were the two windows,
on the west side of the apartment in which I slept.
It was from one of these windows that I had
seen the shadowy damsel gazing down upon this
very grove ; and from this grove, most probably,
had arisen that summoning whistle which had
preceded her departure, and which, I naturally
fancied, had been the immediate cause of it.   But
my observations were hurried as well as my reflections, in consequence of my anxiety to avoid
awaking the suspicions of my friend and his wife.
We returned to the house, where I found several
strangers who had arrived during our rambles.
Among these was Miss Singleton, with whom I
had been threatened.   She was very handsome,
very dignified, well mannered and intelligent ;
but my head was quite too full of the mystery
which possessed it, to suffer my heart to engage
very actively in any independent business of its
own ; and I could see that my fair hostess beheld
me with some surprise, and perhaps quite as
much chagrin, pay but a very passing homage to
the perfections of her favorite.

The reader must fancy all the fun, the mirth-
making, the glee, the dance, of a Southern Christmas ;—the creature comforts in profusion, the
egg-nog, the mince-pies, the hams and turkies ;
the plenty which prepares for any number of
visitors, and the welcome which makes them all
at home.   I did not heed these matters, scarcely

to observe that my friend's wife was not less tidy
and prompt, not less considerate, observant, and
solicitous to please, than she was sensible and
lovely.   Of course, I strove to do my proportion
of the gallantry ; but though, perhaps, sufficiently
successful so as not to betray the presence of
any very troublesome thoughts or cares, yet I
felt the duties very irksome, and watched the
progress of day to night with great impatience.
The evening passed off in whist and cheerfulness.
Mrs. Ashley was my partner in a rubber against
Miss Singleton and Frank, and we rose the con-
querors, though I was compelled to suffer the
reproaches of my partner for having trumped
two tricks which her superior cards already had
secured.   Perhaps, my rebuke would have been
less moderate, had our success been less complete.   I only wonder that my blunders had not
been far more frequent.   It was by a strong effort
of mental determination alone, that I could even
partially withdraw myself from those foreign
thoughts—that shadowy world—into which the
strange visions of the night rose forever to beguile
me.   The faces upon the cards in my hand
seemed still to be those of the haunted chamber.
I could no more play a Queen of Hearts, or a
King of Clubs, without beholding them ; and my
eyes, with scarcely suppressed impatience, were
constantly turning to the hands of the clock over
the mantel, as they seemed to linger and sleep
upon the dotted stages that designated the (then)

slow progress of earthly minutes. At last, the
company began to separate. The lady of the
house gave the signal, and Frank Ashley, little
suspecting how much I owed him for the movement, pleaded a bad headache in excuse for retiring himself a few moments after. You may
fancy the mingled feelings of anxiety and awe,
with which I followed the servant who bore the
light to my mysterious chamber.

CHAPTER VII.

MY SECOND NIGHT IN THE HAUNTED CHAMBER.

"What! doth this thing appear again to night?"
    *   *   *   *   *   *
"I'll cross it, though it blast me!"—HAMLET.

ONCE more within the chamber, and the servant
dismissed. It may readily be supposed that I
strove to muster all the resources of my courage
for the promised adventures of the night. So
deeply had I been impressed—not to say oppressed—by what I had seen—so thoroughly were the
images of the two persons fixed in my mind and
memory—that I retired to bed with a perfect
conviction that something more was to come of
it—that I was to endure a repetition of the same,
or behold the revelation of yet another scene, in
which the same parties should re-appear. I felt

sure that what I had seen had been vouchsafed
for some special object—that I was to become
an agent in some drama of the future, having an
intimate connection with some terrible drama of
the past. Thinking thus, and thus believing, my
next concern was as to the degree of moral
strength with which I should encounter further
revelations. That I should be, a second time, a
victim to the chilling and dreadful sensations,
which, on the previous occasion, had so overcome
my nerves and manhood, I earnestly deprecated
by prayer, and a thoughtful consideration of the
whole subject—by urging my own innocence of
all evil intention, and by the natural solicitude
which I persuaded myself that I felt—apart from
all idle curiosity—to get at the truth in order to
prove myself an active agent in the prosecution
of that justice, the denial of which is generally
assumed to be the chief cause of discontent
among all legitimate ghosts, "revisiting the
glimpses of the moon." My reflections, not to
say prayers, seemed at length, to myself, to be
productive of beneficial effects. I felt myself
strengthened by them, and sternly resolved, what
would come, to prove myself a man in the further
prosecution of the business. I determined not
only to look my visitors in the face, but to speak
to them—nay, if need were, to follow and pursue
them—should they appear—wherever they might
be disposed to conduct my steps. But, though
arming myself thus, by thought and prayer, I did

not forget the usual precautions of a veteran
traveller, but got my carnal weapons also in preparation to assist in carrying out my more vigor-
ous resolves. I had my doubts, all the while,
that the ghosts might be made of penetrable stuff;
and I thought, if so, that the unwarrantable in-
trusion into my chamber, might amply justify me
in the employment of an ounce or two of lead.
My pistols, newly sounded and fresh-primed,
were transferred from my trunk to my pillow.
My dirk lay conveniently on a chair beside my
bed; and all these matters having been arranged,
as much to the purpose as was possible, I proceeded to undress myself and tumble into bed,
with that dogged determination to be brave which
one is never more apt to declare, than when he
himself entertains the most serious doubts on the
subject. I must not forget to say, however, that,
before making this last important movement, I
newly trimmed my fire, put on some extra brands
of lightwood, keenly examined all the windows, peeped behind the curtains, under the bed,
and scrutinized, without finding anything particularly suspicious or offensive, every hole and
cranny of the apartment. I then resigned myself to sleep, with the comforting conviction, that
I had done all that could be done, in the way of
preparation, towards giving the ghosts and myself equal prospect of fair play.

My anticipations were realized. I was awakened, after a certain period, very nearly as I had

been the night before. I was oppressed by a feeling of cold, which seemed to subdue my mind with a painful and humiliating sense of incompetence and debility. The only physical faculty which seemed completely yielded to my exercise was that of vision. I could see, yet my fire was utterly extinguished in the chimney, though I had provided, and set ablaze before retiring, a couple of knotted fragments of the pitch-pine (*lightwood knots*,) which, as every Southerner knows, possess a remarkable power of retaining the flame without being consumed, burning in some instances, where the knots are large and very jagged, for several hours. There was no moon—of that I had made myself sure—and the window curtains being down, as when I had retired, the star-light without, could have very little influence upon objects within the chamber. Nevertheless, there was a light—a sort of vague, misty, vapory brightness, suffused throughout the room, not unlike that which is shed from the moon, through the medium of clouds, which yet render herself invisible. This was sufficient to render perceptible, though still in vague and imperfect outlines, every conspicuous object in the apartment. The light was less strong than on the preceding evening, but was evidently stronger than when I had first awakened. There was the table, and the wash-stand, the chairs, and the inoffensive curtains; as yet, however, I saw nothing which should startle or alarm me; and though I still conjectured, from the unnatural chill which overspread me, that my

4

strange visitors were at hand, I was yet, at the
same time, gratified to feel that my mental energies were in better condition for resistance than
they had been the previous night. I felt awed and
oppressed, it is true, but not with that degree of
incertitude and timidity, which, on the preceding
occasion, had produced, for the time, all the effect
of a complete paralysis. Thus encouraged and
prepared, I was not suffered long to remain in
suspense. My eyes had not been many minutes
engaged in the survey of the chamber, when they
were fixed, by perceiving the very faint and
shadowy outline of the man, gliding along the
the walls, and moving towards the entrance. I
could just discover that the form and carriage
were those of the person of the past night. I
could not question the identity, for the air and
bearing were remarkable. He was wrapped in
the same dark cloak, which, the night before, I
had seen him remove from the walls. His movements were stealthy, and distinguished by the
greatest apparent caution. The woman was no-
where visible. In another moment he disappeared,—in what way I did not perceive, though, as
he had reached the door when I had last seen
him, I naturally concluded that he had found his
way out in that direction. With his departure I
felt instantaneous relief. The oppressive chillness left my frame. My heart beat with braver
impulses—with curiosity and resolve, rather than
any other feelings—and though still reproaching
myself that this spirit had not been shown sooner,

and while the intruder was in the apartment, I
was yet satisfied with myself that it made itself
manifest at last. I bounded instantly out of bed
and hurried to the door. I found it latched precisely as when I had left it. I then went to the
window and drew aside the curtain. All was still
below. I looked out upon the dense and venerable grove, in which, with my friend, I had rambled
that day. It looked solemn as a place of graves.
That grove seemed to me to have its share in the
mystery. I made, in this respect, a sort of in-
stinctive jump to a conclusion, which no process
of ordinary ratiocination could have justified.
The woods presented one uniform brown aspect
of unmeaning and immitigable gloom. There
was nothing unusual, however, in the general
appearance of the scene. The stars were shining in rich profusion above ; but their beams
were utterly wasted in the unavailing effort to
pierce the tops of the umbrageous thicket below.
I turned to the chair on which I had placed my
clothes, and proceeded to hurry them on, as well
as I might, in the thick darkness which now enveloped me ; for, strange to say, a cessation of
the light which had previously been accorded
me, took place a moment after the departure of
the man. To effect my progress, it became necessary that I should lift the curtain of one of my
windows, and avail myself of the slight assistance
which might be yielded by the wan and imperfect star-light. I hastened my midnight toilet
with a nervous rapidity, which rather baffled than

promoted my attempts. Succeeding, at length,
in getting on my clothes, I caught up my dirk,
which I placed within my bosom, and taking one
of my pistols from beneath the pillow, I proceeded
after the spectre, resolving to visit, by night, the
recesses of that grove which lay beneath my
window, and which, during the day-light, I had
found sufficiently funereal. It seemed so naturally
to belong to the ghostly visitation which I had
sustained, that the conclusion was irresistible
which made me take it for granted that my
'ghost' would certainly shape his course in that
quarter. I had some difficulty in undoing the
fastenings of my door, and still more, in keeping
the ancient hinges from betraying my movements
to every sleepless ear in the household. But,
with some pains-taking, I succeeded; and, groping my way along the anti-chamber, reached the
grand passage-way, and finally felt my way along
the stair-case. Here I paused awhile, for reflection. The absurdity of midnight movements
presented itself, at that moment, very strongly to
my mind. The idea of a sober man—at thirty,
—getting up at midnight in December, to pursue
a ghost, seemed, all of a sudden, one of the most
ludicrous of imaginable follies. And, what account should I give of myself, should I happen to
encounter any member of the household? These
thoughts staggered me, and produced a pause in
my determination;—but, for a moment only.
My dread of the ridiculous gave way to the more

serious curiosity which possessed my mind. Besides, if my conduct tacitly admitted my credulity,
it spoke quite as promptly for my courage. It
was evident, if I believed in the ghost, I still did
not fear it. These consolatory considerations
carried me forward. I was soon at the foot of
the stairs and in the basement story. The outer
door I found unfastened—a very common case
with the mansion house on a Southern plantation.
The mere turning of the latch enabled me to behold that dark, mysterious wood to which I was
sure that my nocturnal visitor had retired. Before leaving the threshhold, I strove to pierce with
my glance the close, thick ranks of gloomy shadows by which it was surrounded ; but in vain.
The star-light was exquisitely bright and soft
over-head—the stars were singularly numerous
—but they yielded little assistance to any survey,
such as I proposed to make, beneath the broad
arms and crowning branches of the massive trees
which composed the mysterious grove. The
stillness, meanwhile, was painfully intense. There
was not a breath in the air, not a murmur on the
earth,—no sound or accent, which, on account of
its familiar tone, might commend itself to a human
ear. Cold and silence had everywhere the mas-
tery, and the biting temperature of the season,
strengthened by the leaden weight and gloom of
the hour, added a singular force to the superstitious tendencies of my mind. But these did not
abate my curiosity. Ashamed of the hesitation,

though momentary, which I had evinced, after
adventuring so far, I resolutely bounded off from
the threshhold, and soon found myself enveloped
within the shadow of the patriarchal trees which
formed, as it were, the gigantic entrance to the
gloomy wood, in which my mystery was to be
sought.

Here, I was arrested, and stood in momentary
apprehension and surprise, in consequence of a
new marvel which now encountered my sight.
At the moment when the over-circling boughs
and circumscribing and contracting shadows of
the grove had completely environed me—when
the stars were no longer visible to my eyes or in
faint spots only, and at melancholy intervals
through the brief openings above—when all
promised to be a cimmerian darkness,—I was
astounded to perceive that such was not the case.
The path seemed to clear up before me. The
darkness, like a cloud, appeared to lift, and "a
little glooming light most like a shade," seemed
to rise up in a yellowish vapor as from the earth
itself. This light, without growing stronger,
continued to grow and to diffuse itself until my
vision could take in objects at comparatively great
distances. A faint, glow-worm atmosphere enveloped the trees ; a sort of sickly, yellowish vapor, not unlike in hue to that of the withered
leaves which lay beneath them, seen in day-light
and in the sun-shine. Through the farthest openings, as far as I might, or had need to look, I

could see the same complexional light extending
—a bland, dull efflorescence, such as the moon
might cast upon a chamber, shining through curtains of a faded orange or yellow. It was some
moments before I could become reconciled to this
atmosphere. It seemed oppressive, and affected
my respiration very much in the same manner as
clouds of incense in a cathedral. Besides, there
was some little mental emotion which contributed
to the same effect. This, however, I quickly
overcame. My curiosity had grown feverish;
and I rather ran forward than walked. I suppose
I had gone some thirty yards. The grove had
become more umbrageous. The hazy light
which guided me, now seemed to lie in spots between the trees, which stood out from it in singular relief. Suddenly I stopped, as it were by
instinct. I had made no mental determination
on the subject. The physical nature obeyed an
influence which it was impossible for the intellectual to comprehend, and about which it had
taken no steps in reason or resolve. The chillness returned to me, and seized tenaciously upon
my legs. I was, in fact, frozen to the spot, and
felt so feeble, that I was compelled to thrust my
pistol into my bosom, where the dirk had already
been placed, and with both hands to grasp the
trunk of an aged sycamore that stood just before
me.

The return of this strange influence convinced
me that, though I saw them not, I was some-

where in close propinquity with my supernatural
acquaintance.   But I did not need this feeling to
produce conviction to that effect.   I was already
made aware of it, by that dim religious light
which circulated throughout the spot.   But, if
unnerved, if oppressed, if benumbed and enfeebled,
my pulsation was that of the physical man only.
My mind was perfectly unclouded and even bold.
I had all the resolution which would have enabled
me to put Satan at defiance.   For a few moments,
however, my physical incapacity seemed to extend itself to all my faculties.   I could not speak
nor see.   But these senses, the latter at least,
soon recovered strength.   I gazed suspiciously
around me, and with the furtive glance of one
who apprehends his enemy on every hand.   Near
me, however, I beheld nothing ; and the attempt
to look beyond me, to any distance, was a singularly gradual one.   When it was made, however,
it was strangely enough rewarded.   There, not
fifty yards in front, in the very deepest part of the
grove, and surrounded with some of its most venerable trees, I beheld the woman of my vision—
but not alone !   There was a man with her; not
the elderly man whom I had followed, but one
—a mere youth—a tall stripling—perhaps not
much older than herself.   They stood beneath an
old tree, in a close relation, which amply spoke
for the tenderness of their mutual regards.   His
arm was clasped about her waist, her head lay
against his bosom, and his lips seemed to move,

and his eyes spoke the unequivocal language of
that admiration which knows no law, and is a
custom for itself beyond all control or custom. I
could see their features very distinctly. There
was love between them—love—glowing, living,
unquestionable love—but it was not the love of
innocence. There was the trepidation of guilt,
mingled with the passion which declared itself in
their mutual glances. They frequently looked
about them. More than once the woman started
and gazed around her, while the man, on such
occasions, would draw her closer to his bosom,
and his lips would move as if engaged in the task
of re-assuring her. They leaned against a tree,
which, as I surveyed the scene with eyes of the
keenest scrutiny, I could almost have painted.
It was an oak, more striking than the trees around
it, for it was dead, and decay had already made
considerable progress in the work of its destruc-
tion. It was already disencumbered of all its
branches. Its decay was most probably attribu-
table to the massive ropes of the vine which,
even in its ruin, it was required to sustain. These
clambered about its top, and stretching thence,
threw out a dozen grasping arms which shot off
in as many directions to other trees, some of them
trailing finally upon the earth at a distance of full
thirty yards from the spot where its roots were
bedded. These formed an arching bower over
head, which, during the intense heat of the summer, must have been a superior luxury in a cli-

4*

mate such as ours. It was probably the sufficient reason why it should have been the prefer-
red spot in an interview of young lovers. Under-
neath, the leaves were thick, and formed such a
couch as delights the aching eye and relieves the
fainting form, for which it seems expressly spread.
In short, the whole aspect of the scene, in the
language of the song, presented that of

      " A spot for lovers, and lovers only."

But they were not suffered to enjoy it long. I
had been but a very few moments engaged in the
survey, when something seemed to alarm the
couple in their stolen interview. The woman
darted from the embrace of the man, while he
looked about him as if preparing for danger. But
this did not seem to approach. Still the apprehension of the female was such that she continued
her flight. Her companion followed her, and in
a few moments they had both disappeared, though
in what direction, I was not prepared to say.

I had drawn a long breath, and was recover-
ing somewhat from that stupor which had left
me motionless. I naturally thought my discoveries over for the night, and was about to turn
away from the spot, with the intention of regain-
ing my chamber with an expedition proportioned
to the chilling temperature which I suffered where
I then stood; when something drew my eyes to
another part of the grove, nearer to the house;
and there I beheld the figure of the man whom I

had pursued from my chamber, and whom, from the time when he left my room, I had not till that moment seen. He stood against a tree, and seemed to have been gazing, like myself, at the guilty couple which had just disappeared from view. He, like myself, seemed frozen to the spot where he stood. One arm grasped the trunk of the sycamore against which he leaned as if to support an otherwise falling frame. His features were more distinct than I had before seen them, though I still could not but perceive that, though several steps nearer to me than had been the lovers, (so I may be permitted to call them,) I yet could trace out the lineaments of their respective countenances with far more ease than I could distinguish his. On the two previous occasions, when I had seen him, his face had been a mere outline—an outline that I should easily remember, but still only an outline. I could now see that he was a man who had passed the meridian of life ; but what were the peculiar traits of his countenance had been hitherto somewhat beyond my scrutiny. Under my present survey, I should have esteemed his features to be those of a very good and benevolent person. His mouth was small, and feminine. His nose large; —his eyes of a dark blue, and mildly expressive in tone. The particular language, at this moment, of his united features, was one painful and humiliating to behold. It was the language of utter woe—of a broken heart ; beyond relief,—beyond all hope of relief. Even after the guilty pair had gone from sight, he still continued to watch the spot where they had been. A vacant stare shot out from his eyes, and when this disappeared, and they seemed to re-enliven with consciousness, the return of sense which they exhibited was that of an intelligence far more crushing and harrowing than would have been the unmeaning gaze of idiocy. For a few seconds he maintained the position in which I had first seen him ; one arm clasping the oak upon which his breast was leant, while his head was bent forward, and his unemployed arm dropped listlessly at his side. Suddenly, he sank forward, the grasp of his arm relaxed upon the tree, and he descended, his limbs seeming to stiffen as he fell, heavily to the earth, in which his face must have been buried. I bounded instinctively to the spot, but my labor was taken in vain. The shadowy form disappeared as suddenly as the others, and I was enveloped in utter darkness at the same instant.

CHAPTER VIII.

DAYLIGHT COGITATIONS AND EXPLORATIONS.

It was with some difficulty that I groped my way back to the dwelling and my chamber. Half frozen, I got into bed with all possible despatch, and by that kind provisionary caution of nature, who comes opportunely to the relief of her subjects, and suffers none of them to be taxed beyond his powers of physical endurance, I was soon relieved by falling into a soothing and oblivious slumber. I had no dreams, and suffered from no further disturbance that night. I woke late, but refreshed and strong. My face, as I surveyed it in the glass with ordinary complacency, told no tales that I cared to keep secret. It was as decidedly that of one who had enjoyed

———————"a fair good night,
And pleasant dreams and slumbers light."

I felt that it would defy the keen, inquisitive glances of my hostess, and I resolved that, as yet, my tongue should be equally chary of its revelations. It was really to the disappointment of Mrs. Ashley, as it was to the disparagement of the legendary chamber, that I had no tales to tell,—that I had maintained my ground against the ghosts, and exhibited a degree of indifference on the subject, which confounded her, and really gave a serious blow to that faith in the tradition in which she had been so fixed before. She little knew what a struggle I had had to keep up appearances, and to play properly that part which seemed to be imposed upon me by my reputation of manhood. It was to the real and secret gratification of this feeling of manhood, that I felt none of that mental worry and apprehension

which had followed upon my experience of the
first night.   The fact is a singular one, for which
I have felt myself unable to account, but so it is
—day the second brought with it none of the
mental suffering that came with day the first.
Then, I started at every shadow—half recoiled
at every sound, and drew before the physical
eye every image, however faint, which darted
across the retina of the imagination.   But now,
I was not merely calm—I was bounding, positively elastic.   I felt that I could give myself up
to the gay circle,—chat with the idlest—laugh
with the loudest, and perform all the duties *selon
les regles*, of one of those demi-gallants, who, on
the verge of bachelorism, is yet permitted, by the
grace of dames, to feel that he is not entirely
without the pale of that antagonist state, civil and
moral, which is supposed to be tolerated everywhere, except in the heaven of Islam.   I could
now better perceive, and do justice to, the charms
of the fair Miss Singleton;—and, in so doing, I
evidently put myself a peg higher in the estima-
tion of Mrs. Ashley, at least.   But of this hereafter.   Elizabeth Singleton was certainly—I may
say it here—a very fine woman.

  Though I could not entirely satisfy myself as
to the origin of this great and beneficial improve-
ment in my feelings, in this respect, yet several
reasons might be assigned for the superior un-
concern of my mind, during the second, over the
first, day of my abode at Castle Dismal.   I found

myself, amusingly enough, looking after these reasons. I was more reconciled to the appearance of the ghosts. That was something gained. My curiosity was partially gratified, and awakened to a more satisfactory and hopeful eagerness. Curiosity, it is well known, will overcome timidity, even in minds of the most timid and effeminate organization. But, perhaps, the best reason for my greater confidence and ease, and the utter freedom from annoyance which I felt this day, was the result of my greater satisfaction with myself. I had restored myself to my own confidence. I had plucked up courage to face and to pursue the enemy—and that was everything. It may be, also, that I now ceased to feel anxiety —at least in any extraordinary degree—for the sequel of a story, the continuation of which seemed to be assured me by the recurrence of the visionary forms—the evident progress in the succession of events, and the appearance of a third party on the stage of action.

Well—that day we passed very pleasantly. I was really in excellent spirits—but my gallantries,—what I said, did, and looked, to convince my neighbors of the opposite sex that my bachelorism was not certainly chronic—do not constitute a legitimate part of the present narrative. It would certainly be going somewhat out of my way, were I to relate how I commenced my wooing—how excruciating I became in my attentions to Miss Singleton, and how, in the course of human events, and in consequence of another declaration, quite as explicit as that of '76, Benedict became,—what he will not hint in the present chapter. Sufficient for the day is the evil thereof.

' There would have been a time for such a word, to-morrow."

These things—these hereafters, that creep on

" In petty pace from day to day—"

are they not already written in the chronicle of Hymen. *Revenons a nos moutons.*

———

Amidst all my gallantries and humors of the day,—and, to speak frankly, I was certainly more merry, and more of a ladies man than I had ever thought myself capable of becoming,—I yet contrived to steal away from the group,—and, all alone, to appropriate an hour to the tracing out, in the perfect daylight, of my last night's route among the gloomy intricacies of the mysterious grove. Some curious contradictions occurred to me in the scrutiny which followed. I found,—so I fancied,—the very tree behind which I had sheltered myself, while watching the proceedings of the three. But its size then was more vast and capacious. To be the same, I could scarcely conceive it, unless by making liberal allowance for the exaggerating medium of that strange light, through which, the night before, everything had

been seen, and probably magnified. Assuming
this to be the same tree,—and I really could not
be half so sure of any other,—I next sought, in
the required direction, for that, beneath which I
had seen the elderly man, when he seemed to
cower under the pressure of that calamity, the
character of which I had learned so definitely to
conjecture, from the vague, wild, but closely affiliated circumstances, which have already been
described. This tree I also found. At all events,
I satisfied myself that I could not be very far
from it, on account of the close resemblance of
the other, and surrounding objects, to those which
had stood in its connection during my previous
survey. The only doubt which prevented entire
certainty on this head, arose from the great apparent increase of the space which separated my
place of watch from his. While, during the night,
I had conjectured him to be not more than twenty-
five or thirty yards from me, the point at which
I *now* determined his *then* locality, was nearly
two hundred from my own ; and my farther
examination of the place where I fancied the
two lovers to have been, and which I now
seemed to hit upon with equal certainty, was
very near twice as far as I had fancied it
during the night scene. These discrepancies
worried me a little, but allowances were to be
made in behalf of one judging intervals of earth
and forest by night ; and then, I was not unwilling to recognize the influence of that phantasma-

goria of light, shadow and image, which clearly compassed the entire scene with a charm as fixed and unquestionable as that which envelops the boundary contained within the witches circle. All things in the enchanted ring are deceptive to the uninitiated. The frightful hag, wears, in the sight of Faustus, the image of the one sweet object, the only Margaret that his eyes have ever seen; and the frog which is forever leaping from her mouth—the corresponding image of that loathsomeness with which the fantastic pneumatology of the Germans still couples the delusion, as if for its exposure and conviction, is never once beheld by the deluded victim. I naturally concluded myself to be somewhat under the demoniac influence. If these visions of the past were intended for my sight—if they were meant to indicate what had taken place in bygone periods—then was it but a proportionate effort of Providence, in resuscitating the dry bones of perishing humanity, to resuscitate, also, those aspects of the ancient wood, as they were in the hours which beheld those deeds, the shadowy outlines of which were now re-enacted to my sight. It was no hard matter to persuade myself that the same power which reclothes the dead with all the external forms of life and action, could prepare my perceptive faculties, so as to enable them to take in a corresponding range of vision, which, under ordinary circumstances, would be beyond the power of sight. But, in truth, I did not reason much on these matters, or at the time. My faith had made large strides long in advance of my reason. I found it more easy to believe than to discuss, though I still continued to examine. I found my way, as I have already stated, to the spot where I had seen the tender interview between the young people, whom I naturally conjectured to be lovers. The grouping of the trees around, with one exception, was precisely such as I had seen it the night before. There was the massive grape-vine, with a crooked shaft rising from the earth, and stretching away for twenty feet, with a girth much thicker than my thigh, until it grasped and strangled in its grasp, a sturdy sycamore, which had perished in its folds, and was actually and only sustained from falling by the embrace which had destroyed it. From this, it spread forth other arms, only less large than the parent shoot, which grappled with other trees in turn, bound them together like so many sturdy outlaws chained for exhibition in the market place, and running riot with its thousand tendrils, sent forth on every side in air, as completely embowered the spot as if the great mother artificer had intended the place as a secure and sacred home for our retreat. There was one mighty water oak, which seemed to be a congeries of trees growing together from the earth, and by actual contact becoming welded in the progress of the seasons, which stood over the spot, and which I remembered to have seen the night before. This was the only tree that seem-

ed to have escaped the injurious effects of the
ambitious vine. A few of its smaller shoots had
clambered up its sides, and taken hold upon some
of its outstretched arms, but these did not seem
very tenacious of their grasp, and it is probable
that the expanding arms of the tree, at each gush-
ing upward of the sap in spring, would cast them
off with an ease which would prove the oak to be,
as it appeared, unconscious of its burden. But
there was one massive tree wanting to the scene
—that decayed one, upon which the vine first
clambered, as I had seen it the night before, and
which then directly overhung the bower of the
loving couple, was no longer there. The spot
where it stood was vacant. A little hillock showed whence the shaft arose ; and stretching along
the open tract before it, just where the shattered
bower must have stood,—lay a gigantic bulk—
the decaying shaft of a mighty tree—one of the
largest of the grove,—which had probably been
prostrated fully fifty years. Its fall evidently
carried with it the vine, which trailed upon the
earth beside it, nearly as far as its remains extended, before it was enabled to recover itself, and,
raising its head to grasp with an embrace equally fatal the sycamore to which I now beheld it
clinging. My examination of the wood was not
much prolonged. Beyond what I had seen, there
was nothing farther to interest my mind or excite my suspicions ; and, after a long musing
reverie of all the circumstances, amid the scene

where some of them had taken place,—a reverie which left all things in my thoughts as vague and full of confusion as before—I returned to the house, prepared to believe that farther revelations were in store for me, which would carry out, to their fitting conclusions, the strange narrative which they had so wonderfully begun.

CHAPTER IX.

THE THIRD NIGHT IN THE HAUNTED CHAMBER.

"What is it ? A spirit ?"—TEMPEST.

I FELT, as the evening drew nigh, the approaches of the third night with quite as much anxiety, though with far less apprehension, than either of the preceding ; and the expression of an early intention to retire, which I ventured as we sat around the tea-board, led to the playful remark of Frank Ashley, that the Haunted Chamber seemed to have a very different effect upon me, from that which it appeared to produce on all other persons.

"Hitherto," said he, "those who slept in it, seemed always monstrous unwilling to get to bed. They kept me up here, to my own vexation and the complete discomfiture of my wife, nearly half the night, so that it was with something of a sel-

fish feeling that she resolved to close it up altogether.   You, on the contrary, seem to love the
ghosts.   A taste of them is not enough.   I shall
have to put you in another chamber, else it will
be next to impossible to get you to face flesh and
blood again."

I took occasion, in answering my friend's *badinage*, to profess my great delight with the chamber.   "It was so very snug, so quiet,—the very
sort of antique apartment which should please a
veteran bachelor like myself."

Mrs. Ashley looked at me with an arch smile,
as she caught my glance, while I spoke, fixed
upon Miss Singleton.   The eyes of the latter
were busy with a book of prints ; and those of
Mrs. A. and myself enjoyed impunity all the
while.

"Bachelor, indeed !" she said with a sneering
smile.   "I wonder that, with so much taste, you
should have so little sensibility.   A man should
learn to love, and get himself a wife, if it be
only to escape the imputation of selfishness."

"Perhaps, it would be far wiser to endure the
imputation, while he enjoys the security that selfishness affords."

"Security indeed !" replied the playful lady,
" ah ! we know that that sort of talk imposes upon
nobody now-a-days.   The time is gone by when
ladies' tongues and tempers were objects of terror,
and the affectation of it looks particularly ancient."

" I am an ancient, Mrs. Ashley—you forget—I belong to the old school religiously."

" Then you never get beyond A. B. C. of the heart while in it, and I recommend you to another teacher."

Here she gave a significant glance at the unconscious lady beside her. I looked my despair, but a significant shake of the head on the part of my fair opponent, gave me to understand that she thought that an affectation also ; and, calling for whist, she summoned me to be her partner, adding something about partnership for life, and ' long suits,' and ' hearts' and ' diamonds,' which, though ordinary technical phrases at cards, were made by her to apply somewhat more directly than before, to the subject which she had been teaching me. A grave look from her husband, first at her, and then to Miss Singleton, warned her that she might be carrying the joke too far, and, fortunately, perhaps for both of us, silenced her batteries for the rest of the evening. The hour spent in this way was a very pleasant one. The match was pretty equal—the conversation, neither over fervent nor yet formal, brought out all the parties, according to their several resources, in considerable strength, and one or two incidental references to literature and the fine arts, which were adroitly suggested by Frank, had the effect of drawing from Miss Singleton some very sound and sensible remarks on these topics, very easily and elegantly expressed. There was a quiet grace about this

young lady that particularly interested me, and,
somehow, when I retired for the night, I caught
myself speculating quite as much upon her mind
and manners as upon the probable reappearance
of the ghosts.   With my thoughts equally divided
between these subjects—strangely antagonistic it
must be confessed—the living and the dead—I
delivered myself with perfect resignation into the
custody of that universal gaoler, sleep !

———

The recurrence of my vision was monotonous-
ly same.   I was awakened under very similar
circumstances as upon the preceding night, felt
the same cold, and behaved in very much the
same manner.   At first, I felt overcome and incapable—physically, I mean, for, strange to say,
at the very moment when my muscles were least
willing in the performance of their required duties,
my thoughts were as well collected, and my purpose as clear and rational, as I had ever found
them throughout the most ordinary noon-day oc-
currences.   The man, alone, was in the chamber
when I first awakened to the consciousness of objects.   His person was more distinct to my sight
than ever.   I could now discern his features, and
their precise expression, with tolerable clearness.
I could see that he was terribly agitated.   His
limbs seemed to tremble beneath his weight.   His
features were convulsed.   I beheld him kneel at a
little distance from the foot of the bed.   He was

evidently striving at prayer. His hands were clasped, his eyes were uplifted to heaven, but there was no peace, no hope, no resignation in their glance. All was despair and desolation, and something more. There was a darker passion at work within his heart, and he could not control it. He did not preserve his humiliating position long. It was not the posture for those thoughts which were working in his soul. He started to his feet, struck his breast, and I could see the big tears, slowly forming, gathering one by one, upon his cheeks. They were like the dew drops that are wrung out with the suppressed utterance of the thunder cloud, which denote the volume that burthens the atmosphere which they in vain struggle to relieve ;—a moment after, and he was gone from sight, desperate and with desperate intent.

I bounded in the next instant from my couch, and followed with no more delay than was requisite to cover myself warmly against the severities of the wintry night. A few moments sufficed for this, and I found myself, soon after, once more upon the verge of that mysterious grove which I again discovered to be lighted up from within, while all without was of that glossy, raven dark, such as the faint starlight makes of the sable shroud with which night wraps the unsheltered form of earth. I saw through the long vistas between the trees, with about the same degree of ease and clearness with which one surveys ob-

5

jects through the lone fretted aisles of a cathedral ; the light coming in through windows of
painted glass. I had been in sufficient season to
behold the man whom I pursued as he apparently sped to a station, much nearer than that he
had taken on the previous night, to the place in
which the lovers found harborage. His form
seemed to glide along through the air. Now I
beheld him in one deep alcove, and now emerging from behind some towering sycamore into the
shade of another. Suddenly he stopped, and I
also. I happened, unluckily, to have taken a
course immediately in the wake of his. I had
been seduced by his progress into directly following him, which I should not have done had I been
less impetuous. I should have taken a little cir-
cuit which would have afforded me a better view
of all parties. As it was, I saw not the two objects who seemed to be still within the glance of
the old man. He approached them in a nearly
direct line, between me and their mysterious
bower. - I was meditating, even then, to steal off
to the right hand and regain my place of secrecy
of the past night, when my purpose was arrested
as I beheld the man stoop to the earth. He seemed to grasp something with both his hands—the
object I could not distinguish—but his arms
moved to and fro with an almost convulsive
motion for a few seconds, and then I heard a sudden crack, like that of a limb yielding beneath a
weight of ice. This sound was suddenly, and

with scarce the lapse of an instant, swallowed up
by a crash, and the fall of some tremendous body
to the earth. The spot on which I stood trembled
as with an earthquake. I was frozen to the spot.
Then followed a groan, and with it, almost in the
same breath, a shriek—the shriek of a woman,
expressed in all the voluminous energy of sudden
and immitigable terror. While my heart was
yet palpitating with the excitement of my situation, I suddenly perceived the dim outlines of the
man's person,—more indistinct than ever to my
sight—as he glimpsed beside me, and disappeared in the direction of the house. I had scarcely
drawn my breath, after his passage, when the
woman appeared in sight. She was apparently
taking the same direction, and, from her looks,
evidently much more under the governing influence of instinct, than of will. Her face, air,
action and expression, would have furnished the
most exquisite study for the painter. Her hands
were stretched out upon the course she was pursuing; but her face was averted, and her eyes,
glassy and wild, and almost starting from her
head, were bent, with the keen earnestness of terror, upon the dim spot from which she was flying.
Her lips stood wide apart, the very symbol of
despair and horror,—human, but most unearthly.
Her progress, as she fled, brought her close beside the spot where I stood. But she did not
seem to see me. Unconscious of any purpose, I
involuntarily plucked at her garments as she pass-

ed, but I grasped nothing but the thin air. The phantom was gone from sight. With an impulse which now found my body free for action, I sprang towards the bower in which the mystery lay, but darkness enshrouded me before I approached it, and when I did, I saw nothing but a pale, transparent light, that flickered upon the ground for an instant, like that of a glow-worm, and then went suddenly out.

" God of Heaven !" I exclaimed, with an insuppressible burst of awe,—" can that be a human soul !"

I shuddered with the involuntary reflection, and turned my steps in flight. It was with no little difficulty, and amidst many strange and oppressive apprehensions, that I at length succeeded —groping amidst the weighty darkness which enveloped the woods,—in making my way back to the mansion, and finally to my chamber.

CHAPTER X.

THE DEER-HUNT.——A DISCOVERY, BUT NO DEER.

> " To hunt the deer with hound and horn,
> Earl Percy took his way."
> CHEVY CHACE.

IT was long that night before I could get to sleep. Yet I suffered under the strongest sensa-

tions of fatigue. My mind was too much excited
for sleep. My fancy, vividly active, was peopling
my chamber with dim, visionary forms. When I
did sleep, which must have been towards day-
light, the same images filled my dreams. I once
more found myself in that mysterious grove, in
the track of the spectral husband. His form and
features now appeared more distinct than ever to
my eyes. Hitherto, I had seen him with far less
clearness than either of the two other parties to
this strange drama; but, in my dream, he appeared quite as distinct, the features as individu-
ally distinguishable, their character quite as
strongly written. We re-trod the dim avenues
of the grove, in fancy, as I had already done in
fact. Once more I saw him bend, in rocking
motion, to and fro, but now I could perceive, with
more certainty, the object of his motion. His
hands grasped the serpentine length of the monstrous grape-vine, whose distant folds encircled
the tops of the decayed tree, under which the
lovers were reclining. My dream seemed to
supply all the links which were wanting to my
previous discoveries. I saw the vine as it waved
under his movements. I beheld the old tree as
it yielded to his efforts. I heard the sudden
crack, then the crash, and felt, a second time, the
shock, as the mighty mass descended to the earth.
I was suffered cognizance of more. My imagination supplied the other aspects of the scene. I
saw the woman, as she started from the youth's

embrace, at the first creaking sound of the yielding tree. She had gained her feet as the tree
fell. Not so he. I saw the dreadful event as it
occurred and concluded his fate. He was in a
half rising posture, his eyes cast upward, as the
colossal trunk descended. In the next moment
the catastrophe had taken place. I heard an
awful but low groan, which was lost in the
mighty shock which followed the contact of the
huge tree with the earth. I saw nothing more
of the victim save one outstretched arm, which
was thrust from beneath the ruins—a single arm
—the fingers of which worked with one convulsive motion, ere the whole scene was swallowed
up in darkness.

Much more of this strange vision filled my
dreams that night. The husband and wife were
visible in other and very various situations. But,
in all their features, there was an expression in
no respects dissimilar to such as they wore on
all previous occasions. In the face of the man
was watchfulness and distrust. In that of the
woman was apprehension, which seemed sometimes to amount to terror, wan misery and hope-
lessness. There was a mixture of caution and
cunning on the part of both, even in their most
intimate relations, which amply declared that
active antipathy in their souls, which they yet
sought to conceal from one another. I could not
well say, in what particular situations, after this,
I beheld these parties. There was an incohe-

rence in my vision. The shadows came and went without a purpose, and without a warning. Now, I saw the man, and now the woman, alone. Sometimes they appeared together, sitting, as if at a table, or conversing, seemingly, upon the same bench. But, though intimate, there was no fondness, no friendship, in their looks and performances. At such times, there was a keen watchfulness in the glance of the man, and a downcast apprehensiveness in that of the woman. Once they appeared together, and the scene was the mysterious grove. The woman seemed to be retiring with haste, and in the direction of the house. The man had his arm uplifted as if waving her back. The distance was considerable between them. But none of these appearances served to illustrate the previous history. My dreams sufficed for nothing in the progress of events.

A change came over the spirit of my dream. The spectral forms entirely vanished, and in their place stood the stately graces of Elizabeth Singleton. That young woman was certainly growing in my esteem. I had began to share the partial prejudices in her favor of my gay friend, Mrs. Ashley. To my eyes, in my sleep, she looked particularly attractive. I fancied, too, that she regarded me with more attention, and eyes of more indulgent favor. Such a fancy, as in the case of Benedict, might well enough persuade me to repay such a courtesy in like fashion. I

fancied that I stood over her as she touched the
keys of the piano. Her sweet, deep, sonorous
voice, was sounding richly in song. I began to
feel pleasantly disquieted, when my dreams,
equally of love and sleep, were dissipated by a
stunning sound of mixed trumpeting and howling.
I started up in my bed, and the sounds continued;
sounds, indeed, of trumpeting and howling. My
friend's horn was in full blast at my very chamber
door, provoking a clamorous response by way
of Hibernian echo, from the full throats of no
less than twenty hounds without.

I now remembered that we were engaged for
a hunt that day,—

"To chase the deer with horn and hound."

The arrangements had been made the day before,
with some of our neighbors, and the hunters were
already collected below. My dreams, whether
of the ghosts or of Elizabeth Singleton, had made
me a sluggard ; and Ashley, witnessing the general impatience, had employed his horn at my
door, successfully, in the common dispersion of
the shadows, the sleeps and the loves, which had
kept me from my engagements. The sun was
fairly up, and we had arranged to start at dawn.

"Pon my soul," said Ashley, " the ghosts seem
to give you no annoyance, Clifton. You sleep
as soundly as any of the famous seven. You are
late, and our veteran hunters begin to look surly,
and mutter of loss of time. Colonel Fishhawk is

in a fidget, and even Bess looks squally, as she beholds the coming on of the general squall. Come, man, breakfast is already on the table, and the bucks brousing, whose sides you are to lace to-day."

Mrs. Ashley had her reproaches also. Like a good wife, she took an active interest in all the pleasures of her husband, and was in the habit of giving his guests breakfast at daylight, whenever any adventure, such as the present, was on foot. Elizabeth Singleton was not visible. Had she been dreaming like myself?

"Ah! Mr. Clifton, are you not ashamed of yourself?" was the salutation of my hostess.

"Scarcely!" was my prompt answer; "nor would you, if you knew all."

"What all?" she demanded.

"If you knew what delayed me."

"What was it? I am curious; I am a woman!"

"I was dreaming—or, to speak to the card, and after a poetical fashion,—

> "'I've been dreaming, I've been dreaming,
> Of a lady sweet and fair,—
> And was scheming, and was scheming——'"

"How to kill or catch the *dear*!" was the impertinent interruption of Frank Ashley.

"And who was the lady, Mr. Clifton?" demanded Mrs. Ashley, with an anticipative smile.

"My excuse for delaying the breakfast and the

hunters, Mrs. Ashley, will be furnished by her name, but I can whisper it in your ears only."

"Come, come," said Ashley, "no whisperings with my wife. I'm a monstrous jealous person."

"And did you really dream of her?" was the inquiry of Mrs. A., when I had communicated the name.

"Pon my faith, I did!"

"And what did you dream?"

"Oh! Mrs. Ashley!—"

"Yes, why not? It was a pleasant dream, of course?"

"Remarkably so! There was love in it, be sure."

"I'll tell her!"

"What! and spoil all!"

The appearance of breakfast, and the entrance of the hunters, put an end to this badinage; and the breakfast being quickly despatched, in the general impatience of all parties to begin the day, we were soon mounted, and under way for the scene of sport.

———

There are many famous sportsmen among the hunters in the lower country of South Carolina. The same breed of men is there which furnished the admirable partizan warriors of Frank Marion, in the days of the Revolution. Fellows, famous in the swamp and thicket, great shots, and the most daring riders. For my own part, a citizen by birth, I was neither a woodman nor a rider.

I could cling to my horse, perhaps, under any circumstances, but as for finding my way through brake, bog and brier, I was about the worst possible person in the world for such experiments. As a shot, I was something better ; for, where is the Southern boy, town or country, who cannot make his mark with a bullet, and has not learned to long for the fowling-piece, long before he is able to handle one ?   Like the rest, I could do mischief with such an instrument by the time I was twelve years old; and the idea of deer hunting, and getting a shot at a fine buck in full head, made me even now forgetful or indifferent to the risks of the race.   The clamor of horns and hounds, the shouts of drivers, made a music in my ears, which as effectually drove Elizabeth Singleton from my thoughts, as, from my sleep, the same clamors had driven her sweet song and stately image.   There is something so exhilarating in the hubbub of a hunting party—in the great variety of tongues among the beagles and their masters—that few persons can well resist the intoxicating fury which they inspire.   My pulse bounded in unison with the music of the dogs ; and, putting spurs to my animal, I proved the foremost in cantering off in the direction of the forest.   We had a fine cheering sunshine ; the air, without being sharp, was cool and bracing —a thin white frost had fallen that morning, and the prospect before us was that of a pleasant day, and a stirring chase.   My alacrity called to my

side the hard-favored Colonel Fishhawk. This
gentleman was such an inveterate sportsman, that
the delay, occasioned by my oversleeping myself,
had rendered his approaches to me rather chilling
and formal.   But he seemed to grow into better
humor as he beheld my eagerness.

"You are fond of hunting then, Mr. Clifton?"
he remarked, as we entered the forest together.

"I like stirring exercises, I love excitement,
and, so far, I may be said to be fond of hunting,
but I am not much of a hunter.   I have engaged
very little in the sport; it exhilarates me, and I
am satisfied.   The very cry of the dogs is a sort
of music in my ears."

" So it is!" exclaimed Colonel Fishhawk,—
" there's no music like it.   Talk of your piano
and guitar, your woman songs and bird songs,
but, I say, give me tongue from a kennel of fine
two year old pups, if you want to give me a
music that I love.   That's the music for me."

" A good story, Clifton," said Ashley, who had
ridden up and overheard the enthusiastic eulogy
of the veteran on pup-music ;—" a good story is
told of Fishhawk, and one of his guests.   This
was a Yankee Schoolmaster, whom Fishhawk
employed for his sons—a fellow who had never
hunted a deer in his life, and who had certainly
but an indifferent ear for music.   He had been
on the plantation but a week, when a party
gathered for a hunt.   The Schoolmaster was
among them ; mounted on a huge, rawboned,

grey mare, with a mouth as hard as a grape-shot, and an ugly habit of throwing her head up as if to seek sympathy by contact with that of her rider. The Schoolmaster was not much of a horseman, and the particular animal which he rode, though tame as a terrapin, and quite as slow, promised to give him sufficient employment. There he sat, waiting the signal of departure,—his body as stiffly upright as if it had been skewered up from the saddle,—his legs sticking out at right angles, very much like those of a pair of tongs over a back-log, while his hands were excessively busy in grasping, to be sure of both, the long gun which he carried, and the reins, without a determined grasp of which, he seemed to apprehend that he might be hurried, by his high-mettled steed, into the very tops of the pine trees. Standing thus, and thus employed, Fishhawk, who has been drinking in, with ears for nothing else, the howls, and yelps, and bayings of the pack,—some thirty in number,—turns to the disquieted Schoolmaster, and says, with some abruptness,—' Mr. Standish, did you ever hear more exquisite music ?'—' Music,' says Standish, looking round with no little wonder—' music !— really, sir, those wretched dogs make such a noise that I can hear nothing else !' You should have seen Fishhawk's face ! The sharp, resentful glance of his eye would have gone through any other man. But the Schoolmaster no more saw the disquiet of our friend, than he heard the

music which was thought so charming. Fishhawk could not endure the poor fellow after that;
and, at the end of the quarter, he dismissed him,
with a regret that his ear for music should be so
wretchedly deficient !"

This story was a sort of opening wedge for
the narration of a dozen others, with which I shall
not afflict the reader. It enabled Fishhawk to
open his budget, which was an unaccountably
capacious one, of hounds, and hunts, and horses
—dogs, and their various breed,—in terms quite
as copious, though perhaps less poetical, than
those of Somerville.

We were now approaching the thickets in
which our game was expected. These were
densely umbrageous—a mixture of bay and river
swamp, with thin stripes of pine-land between ;—
little ridges, which, having been kept for several
years from fire, had grown up with a very close
and tangled undergrowth of vines and bushes.
There is no clear chacing in our country. We
have no half subdued deer, in places, half wood,
half park, where a gentleman or lady, on easy
pillion, may follow the sport with the graceful
victim all the while in sight. American forests,
and Southern forests, in particular, are a curious
and various world to themselves ; and he is a
bold and practised hunter, indeed, who can tra-
verse them, even at half speed, without losing a
limb against a limb, or without jeoparding his
eye against some eye-sore, in the shape of thorn

or thicket. Our deer, like the woods they inhabit, are pretty much as nature made them. They are animals, in *feræ naturæ*, for whom legislation has done precious little by way of protection. They are to be hunted, necessarily, after a fashion of our own. A tract of forest, within reasonable limits, in which they are supposed to harbor, is selected as the " drive." The various outlets to this tract are guarded by the hunters. One of these outlets was assigned to my surveillance, and the dogs and the driver—by whom they are followed, stimulated and encouraged,— having entered the thicket together,—our party severally dispersed, each man to his particular post of watch.

The place where I was stationed was on the eastern bank of a very pretty little streamlet ; a branch, which, passing over a dead level, just where I stood, diffused itself over a broader surface than usual, and was separated, here and there, into several little brooklets, that went along, purling and prattling, from thicket to thicket, with a most gentle and innocent levity, until, united at last, in a deeper channel, some fifty yards below. The place was also marked by the ravages of a hurricane, which had occurred perhaps fully fifty years before, but which had left the proofs of its passage in uptorn roots, and overthrown bulks which still gave a marked character to the tract over which it had gone—a sort of arrowy track, about thirty or forty yards wide. The spot was still known, in country parlance, as the "Hurricane." Big cypresses grew on either edge of the streamlet, and smaller ones crowded together knee deep within its placid waters. Clumps of myrtle, and wild vines, which, in their season, were robed with green, glistening leaves, and bright pink and yellow flowers, enlivened the region ; and between my examination of the spot, and my musings upon the ghosts and Elizabeth Singleton, I very soon forgot where I was stationed, and for what purpose. A dreamy languor filled my soul, and though I did not sleep, yet my senses were so completely absorbed in abstract contemplations, that I might just as well have slept, for the good of the watch which I was appointed to maintain over the deer in "Hurricane Harbor."

I was awakened from my reveries by the sudden burst of the hounds, in full cry, almost at my ears. The effect was quite as startling as if the cry had arisen from the opening ground beneath my feet. The wind had been adverse, and the hot pursuit and clamors of the hounds had failed to reach me, until the moment when they broke cover, and were within sight. I started to my feet. I had been sitting on a log. My horse was hitched to a swinging limb some fifty yards behind me. I started to my feet, excited to a most nervous degree. The deer were alongside of me, not thirty paces off, four fine doe, bounding off, and bearing away, to the forests in the rear, with the rapidity of light. Though taken by surprise, and at disadvantage, for a huge cypress stood between me and my objects, yet, to wheel and fire, instinctively, was the work of an instant. I *felt* that my first shot was thrown away. I *felt* that I had not mastered either my pulse or my sight. The second was more deliberate. But, by this time, the distance between me and the flying deer was greatly increased. They were from eighty to an hundred yards off. But I resolved to *tell* this time. I did so. They disappeared like the flash of a star. All were gone from sight in another instant; and, in one more, the hounds had also disappeared—the whole troop, Tray, Blanche and Sweetheart. I leapt upon my horse and followed. There was blood upon the grass—plenty of it—blood from the lungs,—vital blood that lay like so much red froth upon the yellow leaves of winter. I was never more excited. Like Young Lochinvar,—

"I stayed not for brake, and I stopped not for stone,
But swam the Esk river where ford there was none."

I did not swim the Esk river, but I did more— I swam the Edisto, where ford there was none— a broader and deeper, and more rapid stream. I was too much aroused to stop at trifles, and being like young Lochinvar, after *my deer*, I was not to be outdone by that gallant. The dogs and does had gone in the same direction, clean over. The former had smelt and tasted the blood of the

wounded animal and were not to be restrained.
My proceedings were all those of impulse. I
was in the broad stream, my horse struggling in
the current, at a bound, and before I knew where
I was, or what I designed. I had no idea that
the Edisto was within five miles. But, once in,
the shortest way was through. Through I went,
but neither dogs nor deer could I find. They had
probably been less affected by the current in
crossing, and had accordingly gone out at a
point above that where I landed. My landing had
been easy. I do not suppose that I had perilled
myself very greatly in the adventure. At all
events I was not conscious of danger at any moment in my passage, though the stream was black,
bold, and run with prodigious velocity.

But, once on the opposite side, what was to be
done. My enthusiasm had been most effectually
cooled by the water; and, without dog or deer, I
began to feel very decidedly the awkwardness of
my position. I pulled up my horse and listened
breathlessly for the voices or the horns of the
hunters, or the bay of the beagles, but I listened
in vain. The hunters had probably scattered
themselves in search, and I came to the conclusion that the dogs were excellently employed in
munching up the deer which they had taken.
That they had taken her I could not doubt from
the great quantity of vital blood which she had
shed in flight. That she had crossed the river
(if she had) was matter of surprise. If she had

not, the dogs were running still on a wild goose chase. Under any circumstances, it was very evident that our farther sports for the day, were entirely at an end, and the freezing inquiry recurred to me, "what the deuse am I to do? Where am I to go? How get back?"

There were no answers to these inquiries. A deep and mysterious stillness covered the woods around. There was not a bird to be seen hopping from the branches—none were to be heard. Even a squirrel would have been a satisfactory sight, though he could have answered no questions, to my hungering eyes. While I stood bewildered, and quite dispirited, I fancied I heard the baying of a distant hound. I turned my horse in the direction of the supposed sound, and gave him the spur. With some difficulty I made my way through the thicket that grew down almost to the edge of the river. I pressed on for a considerable time, an hour perhaps, encouraged every now and then by what seemed the tongue of the beagle, and had probably gone over a space of two or three miles, when I was brought up by the river, which I came upon suddenly again—a broad, full stream, that spread out, almost like a lake, directly across my path. At the same instant, the sounds which I had supposed to issue from the throat of a dog, were repeated almost immediately above my head, from that of an owl, which flapped its wings at my coming in a lazy flight to the opposite side of the river, where, perched on a rotting gum, it sat glowering at me with eyes in which I fancied I saw quite as much contempt and ridicule, as anger. I was positively bewildered. I had now lost myself. The crooked river, like a long-bodied and cunning snake, had completely enclosed me in its circle, or so completely, that I knew not what direction to take in order to avoid it. My obvious course seemed to go back to the spot where I had crossed it, in order that, should the hunters have followed the dogs, I should meet them there, and have proper counsel what to do with myself; for, to cross the stream again, as I had done before, was now a matter of very chilling annoyance and difficulty to my mind. I now thought only of flats and ferry-boats, and bridges; or in statute language, " roads, bridges, and ferries," as the becoming mode of passage for a gentleman of my condition. The taste which I had of the Edisto water, the strength and depth and breadth of the stream, were all sufficiently well known to me without any farther rash experimenting. But, the attempt to do what I designed, was less easy than I fancied. I failed in the effort even to find my way back to the spot, on the river, which I had left, and wasted another hour in the search of it. I took the track of a horse which proved not to have been my own, and striking finally into a cattle path, found myself after some five miles walking, trotting and cantering, pacing along a pine land ridge, quite removed from all appearances of the river. I was very tired and began to get fidgetty and feverish. My horse showed my discontent. I manifested it by putting my spurs more frequently into his sides than was agreeable to his feelings or creditable to mine, and he showed his conviction to this effect, by an occasional flinging up of head and heels, and a chafing restlessness of demeanor, that sometimes threatened to carry me up against a pine tree. While this lack of congeniality was displaying itself between us, we suddenly struck upon a wagon track, and, glad of any chance of getting out of my present bewilderment, I did not ask to what or whose dwelling it would possibly conduct me, before I turned my horse into it. He seemed equally willing, with myself, to take the present chances in preference to the past ; for, pricking up his ears, with a good-humored sort of acquiescence, he darted readily into the path, and his labored and heavy trot, much to my satisfaction, was changed at the same moment, into a light canter. This, indeed, appeared to show that he knew his way, and reconciled me rather more to mine. " The traveller," says the western proverb, " whose horse knows what he is about, may sleep in the noon-day saddle."

It was the noon-day saddle with me, and rather past it, though I had no thought of sleep. I looked at my watch. It was near two o'clock. The day had become almost as warm as in the month of May. I felt languid and weary, but was still

too anxious on the subject of my whereabouts, to
lessen or restrain the free movements of my horse.
On we went, for a space of two miles, when we
came to an opening. First, we passed a corn,
and then a cotton field ; and, at length, we drew
nigh to the pleasant smokes of a farm house.
There was the enclosure—there the cowpen—
the poultry yard—and there, a hop-skip-and-jump
from the road side, was the cottage ; a small, rude,
but snug log-house, with a broad piazza in front.
In this piazza sat a man. His back was to the
entrance. His eyes were cast down upon his
lap. His position was an awkward one ; and,
from the road-side, I could not account for it, or
conjecture in what occupation he might be engaged. My approach did not disturb him, or
seem to attract his attention. He neither turned
to look, nor betrayed the slightest consciousness
of my approach,—and I concluded that he was
either deaf or asleep. There seemed to be no
other person about the premises. I alighted, fastened my horse to a tree in front, and, opening
the gate, advanced to the house. I ascended the
steps snd entered the piazza without disturbing
him. He slept. I looked over his shoulder.
There was a book open, in his lap. It was the
Holy Bible—one of those cheap, plain quartos
which the art of printing, in modern times, has
made accessible every where, to the hands of
poverty. The volume was opened at " Zechariah,
Chapter IV." the very first sentence of which cu-

riously read,—" And the angel that talked to me came again and waked me, as a man that is wakened out of his sleep." His arms covered the rest of the two pages, saving some fragmentary parts of verse which were here and there visible. I stopped a moment, unwilling to awaken the aged student. His sleep was very sound, and he was dreaming. He spoke a few faint words, and a deep sigh escaped him, that appeared to come from the bottom of his soul, and lifted his chest, as if with a convulsion. He was seemingly about seventy years old. His hair, which was very long and fine, was of a clear unspecked white— white almost as drifting snow. There was a little bald spot on the crown of his head, which was smooth and shining like silver. His garments were neatly, even nicely made, though of the ordinary plain blue homespun of the country. His shoes seemed to have been regularly brushed at mornings—a practice very unusual in the history of farmers in general. These were the observations which I made before I awakened him. This, at length, I did, by advancing in front of him, and gently laying my hand upon his shoulder. He started up quickly, with an air of alarm and trepidation, and looked round him with a glance of apprehension amounting to terror. I receded involuntarily as he did so,—with a feeling of surprise perhaps scarcely less than his own. The features which he displayed to my astonished eyes, —making due allowances for the lapse of years and the effects of time—were those of the man who had made such a conspicuous figure in the spectral visitations to the Haunted Chamber, and the Mysterious Grove of Castle Dismal.

CHAPTER XI.

I can scarcely describe, as I could not entirely conceal, the astonishment and confusion which I felt at this discovery. That he was the same man I had not the slightest question. I could not possibly doubt the identity of the one set of features with the other. They were in both instances, too decidedly marked in all essential particulars— too same in spite of all the variations produced by years and events, to suffer me to reject the conviction which insisted on their oneness. It is true, the person of my vision was a man, only, perhaps, about thirty-five or forty. The individual before me was more nearly eighty. But the likeness had been surprisingly preserved. The only change seemed to be that of a young man into an old one ; and the presence of wrinkles and furrows on cheeks, which, previously, had always appeared smooth before my eyes. Nor were the wrinkles very deep—nor were the outlines much more sharp and angular at the present time, than when they had glimmered before me in my midnight visions. The alteration was by no

means an extreme one—but such only as would
be due to the ordinary progress of years, unin-
fluenced by bitter moods, or periods of great mental suffering. The cheeks were equally full now
as then. The frame seemed even more bulky,
and was quite as erect. The change was in the
hair, which, from being a glossy black, slightly
sprinkled with gray, had become an entire, un-
blemished white. If there was any other visible alteration in the features, it was in their expression,
which now seemed much more subdued—all subdued, indeed, into meekness and gentleness, if not
sweetness and repose—and somewhat more distinguished by incertitude of mind, and a less buoy-
ant assurance. The passions seemed at rest,—
and this constituted the grand difference between
the present and the former man. The agitation
which he had shown when I awakened him,
though evidently that of apprehension, was not
durable, and scarcely to be assumed as the result
of any habitual distemper. It might be only because of a nervous temperament—an impulse,
possibly, of fear, but not a passion—a spark from
ancient embers, not yet smothered in the ac-
cumulated dust and ashes of an abandoned and
decaying heart.

My feelings of agitation and surprise, were far
less easily quieted than his. It required not a moment for him to recover himself, to extend his
hand and welcome me to his habitation. This
he did with the dignity and benevolence of an ancient patriarch. His movements were really very

6

noble ; his manner very pleasing ; his air kind and benignant,—a pleasant smile, rather sad, perhaps, but very sweet, played about his lips, and he looked a grace and superiority so foreign to his dress, and the humble situation in which I found him, that, if there had been no other occasion for surprise, this alone might have been sufficient to deprive me somewhat of my usual readiness of speech. When he spoke, my surprise rather underwent increase than diminution. His tones were those of the high-bred citizen, having all the suavity, sweetness, and freedom from twang and sharpness, which distinguish the large and stationary community. His words were as excellently chosen, without being finical, as if he had been accustomed always to the chambers of a court. Nay, no court, unless thronged with patriarchal and master spirits, could have so spontaneously furnished language so clearly marked by the lofty simplicity of the sacred volume in which I found him reading. It was there that he had gathered his purity, his polish, his perfect English. He had evidently studied the venerable volume with the zeal of devotion. It had impressed itself equally upon his words, his tones and carriage ; and this conviction, which I could not resist, staggered me in the attempt to reconcile the person of my dreams, criminal as he had shown himself, with the seemingly profound Christian who now stood before me. The traces of those wild passions,—that remorseful strife—that uprising of evil purposes, which had distinguished

the man of my vision,—were no longer to be seen
upon his countenance. There, every feature was
marked by a subdued warmth, a genuine humility, and so much indulgence, and so much benig-
nity, that nothing would seem,—so far as mere
exterior expression went,—so different,—so much
at contrast—as the one presence with the other.
The simple start,—the confusion or trepidation
of manner, which had followed his sudden waken-
ing, was all that savored, in any degree, of the
character of him of the haunted chamber; and
this might be due to constitutional timidity,—
which, in spite of years, and any course of moral
training, will be sure to betray itself, in a moment
of surprise, or under novel circumstances.

This course of thinking passed rapidly through
my mind, in the progress of a very few moments.
All my doubts were discussed instantaneously;
and the result was, in spite of all, that there could
be no question of the identity of the two persons.
This, my conviction at the first moment of meeting with him, was that in which I was compelled
to remain. But all my questionings and reason-
ings occupied no such time as has been consumed
—no doubt to the reader's chagrin—in putting
them into words. Meanwhile, I had taken a seat
in the piazza,—the old man beside me;—a servant appeared to take my horse, and preparations
were in progress to give me dinner. A few words
sufficed to account to my host for my unexpected
visit. When, however, I told him that I was the

guest of Ashley, of Eagle-Ærie, I saw, or fancied
that I saw, a sudden change of color in his cheek.
It grew sensibly paler as I thought.   This, however, may have been fancy only, for I was conscious, when making my reply, of an instinc-
tive scrutiny of his countenance.   My eyes were
certainly fixed keenly upon his own; and the
most innocent persons, particularly if at all sen-
sitive in character, can not long endure such
an examination.   But, if the old man experienced any emotion, it did not betray itself in
his utterance.   That was prompt, clear, and to
the purpose,   He spoke of Ashley with great
kindness, and of his wife in the same terms,—
though, he added, he did not often cross the
river, and did not accordingly often visit them.

"And how far am I from Mr. Ashley's now?"
was my inquiry.

"Twelve miles, sir.   It is an easy afternoon
ride—the way is a clear way, and there is a good
bridge across the river, a few miles higher up."

I expressed and felt myself much rejoiced by
this intelligence ; and, having rested, proposed to
set forth at once on my return.   But to this my
host dissented.

"The servant is preparing dinner ; my fare is
humble, but, such as it is, it will be placed before
you with good will.   Do not hurry to be gone ;
you will have time enough to reach the abode of
Mr. Ashley before night-fall."

"But I trouble you;" was my reply. "You have already dined."

"Yes, I think I follow a natural arrangement of the day, when I breakfast at sunrise, dine at noon, and sup at dark. I had dined, according to my usual habit, nearly two hours before you came; but it is not a hard matter to provide fare for the famished guest, when the food is simple; and yours is already cooked."

The servant brought it in as he spoke;—it consisted of a few slices of ham, a couple of fried eggs, the wings and breast of a cold fowl, and a few corn cakes. A bowl of buttermilk was brought from a neighboring cupboard, and I was invited to the table. The old man placed himself at one end, and pointed to the chair which was opposite. When I had seated myself, he broke the bread and blessed it,—standing up the while, and uttering an expressive but concise grace, in the attitude of a patriarch, and with just that sort of real feeling of the office he was performing, which so seldom accompanies the utterance of the ordinary household benedictions. While I ate, which I did with the industry of an Indian, half famished after a long scout, he continued to supply my plate with a considerate perseverance that never suffered me to flag. But, in spite of my hunger and industry, I could not avoid the busy inquiries and suspicious thoughts, which filled and vexed my mind. Every now and then I stole a keen glance up-

ward at my host's countenance ; and with every
glance, became more and more convinced of his
identity with my midnight visitors. There was
so much of fascination in this feeling, that his
eyes at length encountered mine in the scrutiny
which they maintained. After this, I could not
help the notion, that his own evinced symptoms
of disquiet. They now more frequently sought,
yet as constantly shrunk from, the meeting with
mine. He seemed to share in my own fascination. He became a little fidgetty, and, as I
lingered at the table somewhat longer than was
absolutely necessary—some few moments after
I had finished eating—he, rather abruptly, as I
thought, rose, extended his hands, and pronounced
the benediction after meat. I rose accordingly,
and we withdrew together to the piazza. Here,
though still curious and anxious, I contrived, with
great effort, to subdue my curiosity, or, at least,
to avoid any further impertinent examination
of his countenance. He became relieved, and
discoursed freely. There was a religious direction given to all that he said, however foreign
the subject might have been to everything devotional. For that matter, he said nothing positively
of a religious nature, but biblical illustrations,
comparisons drawn from sacred history, a free
sprinkling of the facts of that history, and a mode
of expression which was wholly biblical, distinguished his general discourse, which, after a little
while, became free and easy, and rather fluent.

I contrived to institute some inquiries touching
himself. His extreme health, and youthful expression, naturally justified the inquiry if he was
a native; to which he replied affirmatively.
"Had he lived all his life in that neighborhood?"
This was answered with some hesitation:—"he
had!" I made other inquiries, not exactly of the
kind which I really yearned to make, but which
might lead me, step by step, into proximity with
them; but I soon discovered that he began to
hesitate—almost to wince. His freedom of utterance was at an end. He became reluctant and
almost cold, and, gathering up his bible upon his
knees, continued to turn its pages in a manner,
which, distinctly as words, conveyed his desire
that I should take my leave, or at least forego
my inquiries. Feeling that nothing farther could
be procured on this occasion, or by the sort of
proceedings which I had begun, and, as the evening was wearing away, and I had three good
hours of travel before me, with the possibility of
again losing my path, I determined to make a
graceful departure, before I had irretrievably disquieted my host. I declared my intention, and
my horse was brought out from the stable. The
old man, as if repenting his recent churlishness,
now entreated me to stay and spend the night
with him.

"I am a lone man, my son;" was his remark,
"and the company of the stranger is pleasing to

me.   I have had no company, for many years,
but that of strangers."

"Have you no family, sir?" I quietly asked.

"None!   None!"—with impatience.

"But you have had—you have children?"

"No! never, never!—no children!"

He did not now renew the invitation that I
should remain.   His words, in these replies,
though energetic, were yet without vehemence
of tone or expression.   They were spoken with
seeming indifference, indeed,—and it was only in
their simple brevity, and the promptness with
which he answered, that one might see that there
ever had been any feeling, of whatever kind, con-
nected with the subject in his bosom.   I had no
farther pretence, and, at that moment, no farther
reason, for delay.   I took leave of the old man
with a degree of respectfulness, which I really
could not help but feel in spite of my suspicions,
and which seemed to have its effect upon his
manner.   Though advanced in years, he was yet
evidently full of impulse, and its exhibitions had
been as quick, and suddenly changed, as those
of a boy beginning life.   At one moment he had
been reserved, at the next frank and explicit.
Now, that I was about to leave him, he expressed
the utmost anxiety that I should remain; and the
benevolence of his air and language had all the
warmth, and freedom from calculation, of a
youthful friendship.   I looked back, after I had
ridden from his door some hundred yards, and

he was standing in the porch watching me with eyes that were hooded by his hand from the sun. He turned hastily, as he saw me look back, and re-entered the house. The movement recalled all my doubts. It was made with so much suspiciousness that I could not repress my own ; and I muttered to myself as I went the charitable resolution to probe the secret to its very core, the clue to which, Fate, seemingly, was resolved to thrust into my hands.

CHAPTER XII.

SOMETHING OF WILLIAM POTTER.

In this mood, and with these cogitations, I rode forward with a free spur. Resolving to probe, to the heart, the mystery upon which I had so unpremeditatedly fallen, and revolving in my mind the various modes by which this determination should be executed, the time passed without my consciousness. The mind, fairly occupied with a subject of any importance, or likely to occasion any earnestness of thought, or temper, and it is surprising how short the road becomes—how soon one's journey is at an end! My horse was entering the gloomy avenue to

Castle Dismal, before I well knew that I had tra-
versed half the distance.

My return was productive of a very pleasant
sensation in all the household. My disappearance, and protracted absence, had inspired a very
different feeling. The apprehensions of my friend,
and my friend's wife, and their guests, had been
very considerable ; and the whole plantation had
been dispersed in search of me. One after another had returned, bringing no tidings. Frank
Ashley himself had set out in pursuit and had arrived only a few moments before myself, in increased consternation, as his own search had
been as completely unsuccessful as the rest.
They had lost all traces of me from a spot within
a hundred yards of that where I was stationed,—
in consequence of my taking a route, diverging
from that of the dogs and deer,—allowing myself
to be thrown out by a small dense copse through
which the deer had passed directly to the river,
and through which the dogs had followed them,
—but which, my horse, conscious of his own
greater bulk and dignity, had refused to enter.
The consequence was, that I drove aside,—higher up,—and took the stream fully half a mile
above. My tracks were lost, on turning aside
from the copse, in a small bay, which, for thirty
yards, was covered with water. This occasioned the difficulty, on the part of the hunters, in
tracing my course by the tracks of the animal.
The route which I took through the river brought

me out on the opposite side, something more than a mile above the spot whence the beagles had emerged.

The first congratulations which hailed my safe return being at an end, I discovered that my quondam friend, Col. Fishhawk, had resumed the aspect of chillness and gravity which had distinguished his deportment at our morning meeting. He evidently seemed to regard me as his evil genius. I had delayed his breakfast that morning by my late sleeping—had lost the deer by my bad shooting—and, in the alarm which my absence had occasioned, had so prolonged his dinner hour, that he had grown warm at the delay which had rendered the vegetables cold, and caused the meats to be overdone. I never entirely regained the veteran's favor all the time I stayed in the parish.

But it was necessary that I should give an account of myself. This I did with such sufficient clearness as to make all parties readily understand the history of my route. When I told of my aged host, Mrs. Ashley exclaimed :—

" That was our good old Methodist Parson, William Potter."

" Parson, do you say. Is he really a parson ?"

" Yes, and a very excellent one too, considering the little education he has had. I listen to his sermons with a great deal of pleasure, and feel that they do me good."

"Which is the great test of a parson's merit;— but, does he preach often?"

"Regularly; but not always in the same neighborhood, so that we do not often hear him. Indeed, considering the benefit we derive from his preaching, it is a reproach to us that we do not go to hear him whenever we can. 'Harmony Meeting-house,' where he preaches once a month, is within easy distance; only eight miles from us, and, if you like, we will ride over and hear him next Sabbath."

"Agreed! I should like nothing better. But what is the character of Mr. Potter?"

"His character! Why, very good—particularly good. There's no better man in the world, I believe. He is the most benevolent, the kindest creature I ever knew. But there's Elizabeth Singleton, ask her. She knows all about him,— more than I do,—and certainly is more punctual in going to hear him."

I turned to Elizabeth Singleton. A slight glow crimsoned her cheeks as my eyes were addressed enquiringly, and, perhaps, rather earnestly, to hers; but there was no hesitation in her answer.

"I think William Potter one of the best of men. He is as gentle as a child, yet his intellect is very manly. If he is never profound, he is at least never wanting in good sense. I know nobody I listen to with so much pleasure as himself."

"I shall certainly be pleased to hear him, Miss

Singleton. Your opinion awakens my curiosity.
Will you take a seat with me next Sunday ?"

"With pleasure, Sir :" was her very frank reply, but her eyes no longer encountered mine.

A certain consciousness in my own bosom, the
conviction of a strange, new feeling,—a feeling
that seemed very much like guilt—caused me, at
this moment, to look round at Mrs. Ashley, and I
detected an arch smile upon her lips, while her
eyes twinkled, cunningly, in the direction of her
husband. The next moment they met mine, and
the triumph of her playful malice was complete.
It was very evident that she could scarcely keep
from laughing outright. Elizabeth Singleton was
now looking very demurely, and I could see that
Frank Ashley's face wore an expression of equal
gravity. I could very well understand both him
and his wife. These observations were the work
of a moment. The conversation had scarcely
suffered any pause. Colonel Fishhawk, whose
good humor had partially returned as his appetite
had become appeased, now remarked,—

" Potter is a good preacher and a good man.
I'm sure of it; but I must say that I differ with
Miss Singleton in the opinion that he always talks
good sense. Where can be the sense of a man
who speaks against hunting, and says it's a cruelty
to the dumb animals."

" But does he say that, Fishhawk?" demanded
Frank Ashley, with an affected air of indignation.

" That he does !"

"Is't possible! Shocking! But is it true, Colonel? Did you hear him yourself?"

"That I did, and I came near leaving the Meeting-house. I told him afterwards what I thought of it."

"And what did he say to you?"

"Why, he was civil enough :—so civil that I couldn't find it in my heart to be angry with him. He said he couldn't help thinking as he did,—'twas his conscience worked in him so ;—it might be he was wrong in his opinion, and he left every man to his own judgment and his own conscience. He was bound by the law of God to say what he thought right, and to leave to his hearers to think upon it. He told me he didn't mean to offend me in particular, or any man ; and didn't speak with regard to my doings at all."

"What! you thought he aimed at you, did you?"

"To be sure I did. I was certain of it at first, and had he been any other than a preacher and an old man, I should have said three things that would have hurt his feelings."

"What three things, Fishhawk?"

"Why, what else, but time, place and weapons."

"So, you really thought the old man personal?"

"I should have thought a young one so. He made a long sermon out of it, I tell you; and talked a heap about the murderousness and the brutality of hunting, and about our cruelty to dumb beasts, in general, as if they were not given by God for the use of man."

" For the use, but not the abuse of man," quietly remarked Miss Singleton.

" Nay, Colonel, if Elizabeth Singleton takes arms against you, I know not what will become of you. You will, I suspect, be scarcely bold enough to say the three things to her which hurt people's feelings."

" No! no!—be sure of it;" was the good-humored reply of Fishhawk.

" And yet, Fishhawk, you would incur, as a bachelor, some little danger in saying two of these things to a young lady. The danger would be to the challenger, alone, in such a case. Now, Elizabeth, what think you would be supposed the meaning of an old bachelor who should say to a spinster between seventeen and thirty three,— " name your time and place, mad'm'selle, and I'm your man." What would I give to hear Fishhawk say these words to any unmarried lady of my acquaintance ! But he has not the courage for *that!*"

" No! no! Heaven help me. I hadn't the courage when a youth ; and I couldn't hope for it now. I'm sorry for it, Miss Singleton. I'm very sure I should have been both a better and happier man had I been a married one. Marriage is a sort of duty."

"It is kind in you to say so, Colonel ; but it must be painful to you to think so ;" was the reply.

"And why painful, I pray you?"—responded the sportsman, with some appearance of pique.

"Because I can conceive of nothing more painful in the world to any body, than to be deficient in the necessary amount of courage to do what we yet think right."

"A challenge, by all the powers of Hymen!" exclaimed Ashley. "The least you can do now, Fishhawk, will be to hurt Elizabeth's feelings by saying to her with the utmost solemnity—"time and place, Miss—name it, if you please,—I am your man."

Miss Singleton looked a little discomfitted, but Fishhawk more so. The one took refuge in a burst of laughter, the other in one of champagne, the waiter at that fortunate moment having sprung the cork; and, opportunely for all parties, Mrs. Ashley, in the same instant, afforded a respite, by giving the usual signal for the ladies to disappear. They had scarcely left the table, when I said abruptly :—

"This parson, William Potter,—do you know anything about him?"

"You hear ;" said Ashley. "All concur in telling you that he is a good man and a sensible—my wife, Elizabeth Singleton, and even Colonel Fishhawk, though Parson Potter does score him severely, but not unjustly, about his murderous propensities."

Fishhawk muttered something which was only

half intelligible—something in a tone of dissatis-
faction and defiance.

"Ay, ay ;—I hear all that ; but do you know
anything of his life and history ?"

"No great deal. He is a native of these parts
—has lived here all his life, which has been a
long one, and—"

"Was he ever married ?"

"Yes,—I was about to tell you, that some clue
to his benevolence and goodness may be found
in that part of his history which relates to his
wife."

It may be supposed that I was now all attention. Ashley continued :—

"His wife was a very beautiful girl, very
young, too, whom he picked up some where in
St. George's. They lived together but a few
years, when, suddenly, in a fit of insanity, she
disappeared. The search for her for several
weeks was taken in vain ; when, one day, a rafts-
man, on his way to the city, found her body cast
up on a sandbar about fifteen miles below. To
this day, the bank is called 'Potter's Landing.'
Previously to this, a younger brother of the poor
fellow, a fine, hearty blade, rather dissipated perhaps,—was killed by the falling of a tree somewhere in these very grounds, for you are to know
that William Potter was once overseer on this
place, for Bess Ashley's grandfather. This, I
suppose, is the true reason why the old man

never comes here, though I have asked him a
thousand times."

What a volume did this brief narrative lay
bare to me! Ashley proceeded:—

"These are facts which I picked up from the
neighbors who all love the old man. As far as I
know, he deserves their good opinion; and I can
add my testimony to the rest, in favor of his sermons. He is not only a very sensible preacher,
but sometimes a pathetic one; and though, as I
learn, entirely untaught by the schools, yet no
language can be more chaste, simple and suited
to his subject, than that which he employs. I
wonder you were not struck with this characteristic during the time you were together."

"I was. My curiosity has partly arisen from
this circumstance, and from others which you
shall learn hereafter. But you spoke of a brother.
Did this brother live with him?"

"I really do not know. What I have heard
of the old man has been picked up in the most
casual manner. I was interested in his preaching and general conduct, as, indeed, every
stranger must be; for it is evident at a glance
that he is quite a superior person to the ordinary
rustic, or the ordinary preacher of the country;
but beyond an occasional question of some of the
neighbors, I never enquired very closely into his
history. Have you heard anything that makes
you so curious?"

"Nothing," I replied, with some precipitation;

and after a few remarks from Fishhawk, generally confirming what had been said by Ashley,
the subject gave place to others. The Colonel
was better pleased to discuss the fortunes of the
day, which, however, gave him very little pleasure.

"You must have been asleep, Mr. Clifton," he
said to me, with some severity of manner, "to
suffer those deer to get by you so completely. I
only wonder they did not run over you. 'Hurricane Harbor' is a complete valley—a sort of
channel. Had it been running water, instead of
deer, you would have been drowned."

"As it was, he incurred some such risk by his
own running. Had the river been a little more
full, Clifton, you might have been landed, without
your own volition, where Mrs. Potter was."

"Yes, that was the maddest of all chases,"
growled Fishhawk, as he rose to depart.

"Well, but Fishhawk, what *chases you ?* Will
you not spend the night ?"

"No, your house is haunted, they say, and I
believe in ghosts."

"Oh! shame! Why, here's Clifton who has
been sleeping every night in the haunted chamber
itself!"

"Have you, Mr. Clifton ?" inquired the hunter,
turning upon me with some quickness, and with
a more respectful expression than was usual in
his countenance when he addressed me.

"I have, sir !"

" And seen nothing ?"

I hesitated ;—I could not help it ; and he exclaimed :—

" He has, by Saint Jupiter ; I know it. You
can't deny it. You can't deceive me. I'd bet
five hundred to one that he has seen the devil, or
something like it."

" Not so bad, Colonel, but I have seen something, and if you will only stay to-night, I will
freely give up my chamber to you, that you may
share my experience with me."

" The d—l take me if I do ! No ! no ! my
good fellow,—none of that ! The living are
enough for me. I have no wish to know anything about the dead. But I'd like to hear. Let
us know what you have seen."

" No ! no !" I replied coolly. " If the thing's
worth knowing it's worth seeing. I make you a
fair offer. I'm not selfish. Stay and see for
yourself. You shall have the chamber. "

" Not for fifty devils !" and the worthy Colonel
buttoned his coat to his chin, and made a hasty
stride towards the door.

" Why, Fishhawk,"—said Ashley,—" you look
discomfitted—as if the devils were already upon
you. Stay ! when are we to hunt again ?
There are two or three first-rate *drives** down by
Hallam's Quarter."

---

* Deer-ranges, of a form sufficiently compact to admit of
their being partially environed by the hunters, who occupy

"I thank you, but I can't say now. We have so little luck now-a-days,"—looking at me,—"that I scarcely see the use of it, and there's no sport. I believe Parson Potter has put a bad mouth upon the deer."

"The hunters rather! But you persist in going?"

"Yes! I must. I expect some company at Buckhead, from Beaufort."

"Then you will hunt. You can't help it. Those Beaufort fellows will go the death upon a deer."

"Yes! when they've done up the devil-fishing—which they're like to do in short order if they keep on at present rates. Those Elliotts thereabouts, ought to be indicted. They'll depopulate all the waters of St. Helena!"

"And the woods too! They have a knack at all sorts of wild sports. I wish they lived alongside of us. I'm very sure, Eagle Ærie would then be Castle Dismal no longer.—But you will go!"

"Ay, ay!"

"We'll meet at 'Harmony Meeting,' on Sunday, I suppose?"

"I reckon, if nothing happens. Adieu! Good bye, Mr. Clifton, but take the advice of an old hunter at parting. Never again go to sleep on

---

some two or three sides of the range, while the *driver* and the hounds press the deer from the other. *Drive*, taken from the fact that the deer are driven through it upon the hunters.

your stand. I've known a man that was horribly hurt who did so. The deer nearly run through him. I'll be glad to see you at Buckhead Hunt, on Monday next, to dinner, or any day that may suit you after that. If you can spare time to spend a week with me, I shall be very glad, I assure you,—though I won't promise you to *drive* that week."

"Thank you, Colonel, very much. I shall certainly visit you before I go to town; and, if I can, will dine with you on Monday. You are justly severe upon my hunting;—but you will admit, at least, that I have some taste for pup-music."

"Ha! ha! ha! Very good—yes, yes—that I allow," replied the veteran somewhat softened. "Come and see me, and we will try a hunt. You are yet young. You will do better with practice. Something may be made of you yet. Bring him, Ashley. It's not too late for him to learn."

The horn sounded, the hounds set up their clamors, so grateful to the hunter, and in a few minutes more, Colonel Fishhawk might be seen, erect as a tower, and dashing away at full gallop, on his famous charger, whose pedigree he was wont to trace back to the time of William Red Head of England.

CHAPTER XIII.

THE INVOCATION OF A NEW SPECTRE.

WHEN he was gone, Ashley, whose impatient inquiries could scarcely be restrained, said to me:

" Clifton ! you have deceived me ! You have been annoyed in the Haunted Chamber. Your face betrayed it when Fishhawk put the question."

" It is true, Frank !"

" Ah ! faithless ! But what have you seen ?"

" Do not be impatient ;—I will answer this question to-morrow. I have been surprised—annoyed—alarmed, perhaps,—made very curious—still more anxious—and feel myself, at length, on the eve of a strange discovery. But, press me for no explanations now. I will reveal every thing to you to-morrow. Meanwhile, say nothing to your wife to make her either suspicious or apprehensive. Subdue your features as well as your tongue. I now tremble with fear lest any imprudent revelation may deprive me of the clue which, I fancy, is already in my hands—may weaken my assurances, and baffle me in the prosecution of my inquiries at the important moment."

" Tell me one thing, at all events. Has William Potter anything to do with it ? It seems to me now, that, somehow, you contrived at dinner, that everything that was spoken should relate to him."

"It has! But ask me nothing further. You do but disturb and distress me. Let me have only this one night, and I trust to tell you everything in the morning. Nay, I think it likely that I *must* tell you then. I shall probably need your assistance."

Though earnest enough in my expostulations, I had some difficulty in quieting the eager curiosity of my friend. I succeeded at last; and, smoothing our features as well as we could, we joined the ladies in an afternoon ramble. How we spent that afternoon—what was the kind and tenor of our chat—need not here be particularly written. Enough, that Ashley and his wife paired off on some domestic exploration—something about poultry, and poultry houses, and the fatality just then prevailing among the geese. I, meanwhile, unconsciously enough, became the companion of Elizabeth Singleton. Gradually, we went together—leaving the inevitably-paired to themselves, as a matter of course. I cannot say that it was with equal unconsciousness that our mutual steps inclined to the shadowy and grateful solitude of the mysterious grove. We wandered through its solemn paths, musing upon their secluded beauties, and conversing upon the subject of our several musings. This region had been a long known and favorite one with her.

"I feel at home here," she said—"the peace of the spot is grateful to me. The awe which it inspires, and which keeps away others, seems to invite me here,—and sitting upon yonder fallen trunk, I am something surprised by nightfall, without feeling even then, disposed to return to the house."

" Let us walk thither now."

The dismembered and overthrown trunk to which she pointed, was that massive shaft which I have already made known to the reader, as having so large an interest in some of the more terrible events of this narrative. We soon reached it, and sat together upon it.

" This grove has been trodden by those who felt, and thought, and loved, an hundred years ago."

" Longer I suspect," she replied. " Are you one of those who deny all sensibility to our savage predecessors ?"

" Far from it ! They had their loves as certainly as their hates—their fears as well as their hopes. The season of their youth was doubtlessly one of sentiment—such sentiment as belongs to the affections in an inartificial condition—not the warmest, not the tenderest, perhaps—but unselfish as ours—perhaps, less selfish,—and which prompted frequently to great self-sacrifice, and equally great mental suffering."

" But you think it never survived the period of youth ?"

" Scarcely ! The brutal necessities which distinguished their maturer years, and which was inevitable from their condition, must have been certainly fatal to all the delicacies of feeling.

7

The roughening processes to which abject necessities condemn the heart, soon effects its entire callosity."

"And yet," she answered, "I should be disposed to think that the very exercise of the sensibilities up to a certain period, would render them too strong and active, to make it easy for any course of subsequent trial and distress, to subdue entirely. I am disposed to think that the callosity of which you speak, is rather more likely to assail the heart whose feelings are unexercised, than that which is. The still lake is sooner frozen, than the running river. The sea never suffers itself to be fettered by such bonds. I fancy I meet daily in the society of the civilized with individuals whose sensibilities are utterly dead, from the refusal to exercise them, as we are told that the muscle disappears from the arm which is left unused."

I answered abruptly,—for the manner in which the question was put disquieted me.

"And think you, Miss Singleton, that the young lady who never loves, who has no visible ties,—whose affections are unexercised—is finally incapable of loving?"

"No, certainly not," was her prompt reply,—"for in the first place, she always loves, she never ceases to love. Nature provides against that."

"How?" I asked with some surprise. Her reply was ready.

" Your error consists in the assumption that she does not love because she has no visible ties—no engagements—no constant struggle of heart in and heart out, with some neighboring youth—a play and exercise of the affections which is equally common-place and unnecessary, for the maintenance of the affections. Nature provides, in order that the sensibilities should always be kept in activity, that she should love a mental image—an ideal of perfection as it appears to her,—and when she assumes visible ties, all that her heart then performs is the clothing of its ideal with humanity. Your poets, who are never without a sweetheart in the name of a muse, have long since illustrated the natural law in this respect by their own practice."

" Anch 'io son amante !"—I involuntarily exclaimed, as she gave utterance to an opinion which, on the instant, struck me as equally pleasing, plausible and novel.

" What !" she said, while I could observe a slight heightening of the color on her cheeks—" could you entertain any doubt of this ?"

" I have always doubted it until this moment !"

Whether it was that something in my looks or in her own thoughts disturbed her, I know not, but she remained silent, then suddenly rose to depart. I walked on by her side in silence. New emotions were struggling in my heart. Were there any in hers? But what was her heart to me? Why should I trouble myself with such a question? Yet I did. I found myself disposed to ask it no less than a dozen times on our passage to the house, which we at length reached without having exchanged a single sentence. And yet, in all probability, the interchange of sentiment between us was never more close or active than during those silent moments of our progress. The ghosts of the grove were half forgotten in the partial awakening of a new spirit which now began to divide my thoughts, in some degree, with the former. Was it to be laid, like the former, by revelation? With that inquiry, I began to tremble.

CHAPTER XIV.

FOURTH NIGHT IN THE HAUNTED CHAMBER.

I PASS over the events of the evening. Let it suffice for these, that, by this time, my instincts carried me to the side of Elizabeth Singleton in a manner which, I could already see, was very agreeable to my hostess. We discussed engravings together, and this practice is very favorable to the discussion of one's neighbor. We sat contentedly together over the war of chess as spiritlessly carried on as it was protracted. We began, at length, to expect the attention of our mutual eyes, to the several objects which interested each, as a matter which familiarity and custom had rendered something of a duty. We sat up till a later hour than usual—all parties seemed disposed to linger,—and yet there was little or no conversation. I was instinctively reminded, by this expressive forbearance, of the beautiful passage, so true to nature, in which, by inuendo, Francesca tells us of the discovery of her own secret :—

" Quel giórno più non vi leggémmo avànte."

The hour is late. I am once more in the Haunted Chamber. Frank Ashley has taken his departure. He clung to me to the last. He would have spoken, even within the mysterious precincts, of the awful subject which oppressed us ;—but with my finger on my lips, I resolutely enjoined his silence. His footsteps no longer sounds upon the stairs. I am at length alone, The silence is very deep—very impressive and solemn. The ear, pained with its intensity, seems itself to whisper. Can these murmurs which it sends forth, be the whispered utterances of some immortal spirit, hovering beside, and seeking, how faintly, how vainly, to inform me of some terrible but necessary truth ? A spirit, suffering possibly in the agonies of a punishment, adapted by its intense superiority over all other forms of pain, to its superior and immortal condition ? My hair rises with the thought, and stands up, clammy and bristling ;—my skin crawls—my heart beats and bounds, as seeking escape from the frail tenement which keeps it in, but cannot control. With a shiver, I sink upon my knees, and invoke, in half broken and frequently interrupted prayer, the protection and the forgiveness of God ! Half strengthened, I arise, throw off my garments, with uncertain fingers, and shroud myself in the coverings of the couch, with a boyish feeling of partial security.

———

The intensity of my anxieties baffled my purpose of sleep. I kept wakeful a miserably long time—that seemed much longer in consequence of my anxieties—excited by every whisper of the wind—by my own pulsation—by the heavings of the bed clothes, which rose and fell with the deep heavings of my own breast. The night is a period which deprives manhood of half its strength and courage. The best of us, the very bravest, feel, at times, and under the pressure of sympathetic circumstances—its intense darkness and awful stillness, weighing upon us like a form of vague and indefinite danger,—the more indefinite, the more terrible. The miserable vanity of man makes him ordinarily deny this. There is nothing which he so much dreads to be suspected of as credulity. To be counted credulous is the

most cruel blow to his self-esteem. He is flatter-
ed when accused of scepticism. His poor vanity
rejoices in the imputation of unbelief. To ex-
press a want of faith, with weak, vain minds, is
equivalent to the assertion of an independent
thinking. The persons who have just enough of
knowledge for pretension, are the very last persons to believe anything beyond their present
attainments. To tell such persons of a new
truth, seems to them very like an imputation upon
their understandings. How should anything be
new to them—those world-wise, with whom all
wisdom is very sure to perish? Hence, they
always encounter new suggestions with hostility,
derision and doubt. They become thus committed against truth, interested in stifling it, and
sworn enemies to the discoverer. These are the
persons who are generally most active in the
world's business; and hence it is that the progress of discovery is so slow. Such persons are
always banded together to resist it. Where you
know a man of moderate understanding and in-
vincible self-esteem, it is ten to one that you will
find him—whatever be the subject of dispute—in
the ranks of the incredulous. It is fashionable
with this same spirit of self-esteem to disparage
the claims of the spiritual world. Science, so
called, that coldest and vainest of all modern
pretenders, is particularly hostile to everything,
and every thought, which you cannot analyze in
the crucible, or estimate by the square and com-
pass. Its professors believe nothing which they

cannot see and feel.   Need we add that they
know nothing but what is kindred to their own
eyes and fingers.   How well do they deserve the
scornful judgment of Wordsworth :—

> " Whose mind is but the mind of his own eyes,
>   He is a slave—the meanest we can meet."

Ghosts are the particular subjects of scorn with
these grave seignors.   Their laugh is ever loudest
when the topic is but mentioned.   But see them
at midnight in their chambers.   Let their dreams
but conjure up awful phantoms, and their souls
are quite as susceptible of terror as was ever the
soul of the Crouchback :—

> " Shadows to-night
>   Have struck more terrors to the soul of Richard
>   Than can the substance of ten thousand soldiers."

Their instincts justify the popular faith in this
respect, precisely as the instincts of all tribes and
nations are sufficient, without any other revelation, to declare the existence of a God.   Not one
man in a thousand is superior to these instincts,
and of the million that laugh the phantom to
scorn, while in the crowd—while encouraged in
the daylight—not one but feels the awful conviction creeping through his blood, if alone, at midnight, in his chamber, awakened by some terrible dream, or some harrowing sound or circumstance.

I doubt whether I am feebler in this respect than
most persons.   I have not usually thought myself

so. Nay, prior to my visit to Castle Dismal, and my experience of the Haunted Chamber, I was, perhaps, one of those to laugh the loudest at any grave stories of this nature. I was now painfully aware of the difference. I was no longer so strong, though, possibly, not less courageous than before. As I have already mentioned, my anxieties baffled sleep. I strove for it in vain for hours. My expectations were terribly excited. Every thing alarmed me. I fancied the approach of startling shapes; I started in the belief that one was whispering at my head. I remained in this fretful, feverish condition, until my physical man grew perfectly exhausted, and I sank, at length, into unconsciousness.

It is probable that I had not slept many minutes when I was awakened. I was roused by the usual symptoms. My extremities were cold. I opened my eyes upon an imperfect light which was equally diffused throughout the chamber, and which, so completely was it in contrast with the previous uniform darkness, was almost painful to my eyes. But there was no glare, nor was it possible to discover whence it could proceed. I immediately recognized it as that pale, yellow, sepulchral sort of gleam, which had always before accompanied my supernatural visitors. For these I looked earnestly; but, for some few seconds, I was only conscious of a cloudy, indistinct group

7*

that occupied the remotest corner of the chamber. When this resolved itself into form, which it did after a brief period, I could distinguish the outline of two persons, but, either because of my excited nerves, or of the imperfect condition of my vision, it was difficult, for a longer time than usual, to determine between them. There was movement and action—commotion—a stir which I could see, but which I failed utterly to appreciate. At length, however, one of the shapes darted forth, I may say, from the cloud. The obscurity of the whole space was that of complete cloudiness. The figure was that of the woman. Her motion was convulsive; her action was passionate in the last degree; her eyes dilating as if starting from their sockets; and she rushed towards the bed where I lay, wringing her hands violently. She came so nigh to my couch that, had she been tangible, I might have grasped her with my hands. The other figure did not approach, though he had become more discernible. I concluded that this was the man, the husband, as I had supposed him; but I could distinguish none of his features. There was the outline of the man only, muffled in shadow, from which I could now and then perceive a hand thrust out. What was the object of this movement I could not say, but I perceived that whenever it took place, the woman seemed to shrink and cower, as if under the influence of a more than mortal terror. At length, at one of these exhibitions, she rushed, as if under some

fatal fascination, towards the object whose movements seemed thus to distress and alarm her, and,
when I fancied she was purposing more closely to
approach it, I beheld her turn aside and dart
through the door, wringing her hands, the while,
with increasing violence. Her face, which I saw
with singular distinctness, was livid with fright
or pain. I fancied every moment that the living
balls would burst from her head, they were so
dilated and fiery;—and, what with her white teeth
gleaming ever through her parted lips, which
were pale and quivering, her phrenzied action,
her attitude, bending forward, arms stretched out
and hands violently wringing each other,—I could
not have conceived a picture of a more absolute
despair and self-abandonment. When she disappeared, the other shape emerged from shadow,
and I could now distinguish it clearly to be that
of the man—William Potter, the preacher as I
now believed it,—for the resemblance was more
decided to my mind than ever. It was not the
face of the venerable man I had lately seen—not
the William Potter subdued by age, softened by
religion, meek with the decline of wasted passions,
and humbled in earthly hope, in due proportion
with the acquisition of hopes of a far superior
kind—but it was William Potter, the mere man,
crushed in his human hope, bitter with the defeat
of mortal passions, suffering from the first tortures
of earthly remorse, and equally divided between
feelings of hate and suffering. If the face of the

woman denoted a terrible strife in her soul, that of the man was indicative of one scarcely less violent. A moment only was I allowed to glance at those agonized and fearful features, which, though full of anger and misery, were yet quite as full of incertitude. I now saw that his fingers clutched a knife—that his look was threatening—that his eyes were wild with an expression that shewed how completely his passions had escaped the restraint of his reason. I had barely time to note what I have described, when, with a threatening gesture, he darted off in the direction which the woman had pursued.

I could not rise to follow. I had the will for it, but not the power. My energies failed me, and my resolve,—and, though chafing with myself that I did not stir and set forth, I yet clung most tenaciously to my bed. But I had no need to follow. After a brief period the woman re-appeared. She was alone. She re-appeared, but she was no longer the same appearance. The entire expression of her face had undergone a change. The passion was no longer in her eye, or it had become fixed and frozen there. The features, if not passive, were immovable. The hand of death was upon them. A stony fixedness was in her eyes,—they were glazed over, and set. Her complexion was ghastly pale. Her arms, no longer extended—no longer in action, hung listless at her side, and pendant in like manner, drooping as if with their weight, her long thick tresses hung from her shoulders, trailing almost to her feet, and seeming to drip with water. I was instantly reminded of the story which I had heard the day before, of the supposed manner in which the wife of William Potter had perished. Certainly, the tale, so far had undergone the fullest confirmation in my nightly visions. But I was not to be permitted thus coolly and deliberately to speculate. My impressions were to be of a character, too terrible and acute for mere thought. The figure approached me, bent over me, with the most mournful vacancy of expression, while, lifting her long hair, she seemed busy in the task of wringing out from its voluminous masses, the water with which they were surcharged. This she did, while gazing fixedly upon me,—fixedly—with such a glance of imploring earnestness, that I felt the struggling breath rising in my throat, and almost stifling me. I spoke—I scarce know what I said,—but I feel that I must have spoken as if addressing the dead, and proffering assistance. My words seemed to me to be as follows,—but I cannot be sure of them.

"Speak to me—tell me what you would have —what can I do for you ? In the name of God, speak to me !"

Her eyes seemed to regard me with a gaze, equally fixed as before—more intent, but with a deeper meaning. It did appear to me, as if the poor soul, struggling through the dim obstruction of death, was anxious to understand my purpose, or did understand it. But no answer was returned to me. By this time, I was sitting upright in my bed. Her face was almost upon a level with mine. My extended hand might have smitten it. But I lacked the feeling and the courage for such a movement.

"Speak to me, woman!" was again my language. "Say to me how I can serve you. Tell me of your wrongs. Has William Potter—"

With the words, the figure seemed to recede. The hands were dropped once more at their sides. The face grew ghastlier, and finally more indistinct, and at length the whole outline melted into the thin, grey atmosphere of the apartment, which, in a little while, became exchanged for the dense and unmitigated gloom of the most vacant and cheerless midnight. That night I saw no more visions. I had seen enough to keep me wakeful, and it was only towards daylight,— as nearly as I could conjecture,—that I was soothed by the sleep which I had so long and so vainly solicited.

CHAPTER XV.

"With fiery breath
That snuffs the scent of blood, pursue this son,
Follow him, blast him in the prosp'rous chase."
THE FURIES.

I WAS awakened, ere I had well got to sleep, by the entrance of Frank Ashley. His looks betrayed concern and curiosity.

"Somehow," said he, "I have not been able to sleep, thinking of you and what you have told me. You have excited my curiosity so far that it has become distress. Tell me, have you seen any thing to-night? Have you made any discoveries?"

"I have;" was my reply. "Keep still, and listen to me. I will tell you all, as I fancy that I have seen quite as much as will be vouchsafed me."

I related to him what has been already related to the reader. Indeed, I could not well have kept the secret much longer, having a single friend to listen. I need not dwell upon the surprise and astonishment of my friend. Of course I enjoined him to secrecy.

"Do not even tell your wife, Frank."

"No, certainly not."

"For several reasons. It may be a dream."

"Yes, it may be—to be sure it may be a dream

—but, certainly, a devilish coherent one. A sensible dream, I may say."

" Very much so,—but still, when the matter interests a man who stands so well in the community—so beloved by all,—as William Potter."

" True, Potter's a good man,—but,—it's very strange you should see the woman wringing the water from her hair,—his wife being drowned you know !"

" Yes, but you will recollect I never saw her do that before the last night, and yesterday, for the first time, you apprised me of the fate of Potter's wife."

" Sure,—very true,—and yet—"

" There's something in it, nevertheless. The coincidences are too numerous, the events too closely allied, too dependent upon one another for mere conjecture. It is *not* such stuff as dreams are made up of. Besides, there was something in the deportment of William Potter, when I met him, the other day, which tends more than anything besides to impress me with the truth, in more or less degree, of these circumstances. Frank, I am determined to see Potter."

" We will ride over this morning, after breakfast."

" Be it so,—but, Frank, remember—mum's the word."

" Oh ! to be sure."

" It would be shocking if such a story should get abroad. You must keep it even from your wife. Can you—are you strong enough for that?"

"Am I not! Do you doubt!"

"I rather fear,—you are such a good-natured fellow!"

"Pshaw! You know me not. I'm as close as a mouse-trap."

"And as easily seen through! Come! Look a little less mysteriously, or she will probe your very heart till she will find out your secret. Your face is just now that index to a tragic volume, of which the poet speaks. See if you cannot compose your muscles as I can mine."

"Doubtful! I envy you that faculty. You have worn the mask famously. I should never have stood these sights so long. But, stir you! All are up below, and no good housekeeper, you know, likes to wait for breakfast. I will go down and report you as forthcoming."

"Remember! mum's the word," I said to him at parting.

"Oh! yes, mum!"

Mum indeed! His wife was in possession of the whole story before sunset. But this hereafter.

As soon as breakfast was despatched, we were mounted, and on our way to the cottage of William Potter. The task before me was a painful one. Taking the form of duty, its outlines and

objects were not very obvious to my own mind.
Here was a man against whom I entertained the
charge of murder,—and on what authority?
That, no doubt, which a sober court of justice,
and a well instructed jury, would consider the
baseless fabric of a vision. And who was the
supposed criminal? One of the most reputable
men in the country—a minister of the gospel—
beloved by all—held in singular esteem—known
for his virtues,—not known, not suspected even,
as guilty of any, the smallest vices. A thousand
barriers of improbability rose in the way of my
suspicions. But, even supposing them well-
founded—supposing that, once upon a time, in
his hot youth, he had committed the crime with
which I was prepared to charge him—was his
repentance nothing—the long years of virtuous
performance which had passed since then—time
having mellowed and subdued the stains upon
his hands, while prayer and pentience had oblit-
erated their impressions from his soul? Why
should I disturb the few remaining years of his
protracted life? Why wrest from him the good
name and holy repute, and universal respect,
which he now enjoyed? Nay,—even were it
proper that I should do this,—suppose him stub-
born—suppose he met my story with scorn and
denial—what should I say—how support it—to
what conclusive evidence appeal, that the truth
should finally be established? I saw and suggested these difficulties to Ashley. We both felt

their force;—but, when this was acknowledged, I felt an impelling something within me, which forbade that it should have way—which forced me forward—which seemed to say, " thou *shalt* speak—he *must* hear. Do then, without question, even as thou art commanded."

I obeyed the voice ! I could not otherwise ; and, impatient of the time consumed upon the road, though riding half the distance in a smart canter, we at length found ourselves at the cottage of William Potter. At our approach, the door opened and he appeared at the entrance. We alighted, fastened our horses to a tree, and ascended the steps, in doing which our mutual eyes caught a glance at his face, and were instantly struck with the emotion which it evinced. It was very pale—his lips trembled, and his frame tottered. He made a step towards us, but no more,—and stood fixed, motionless, until we ascended, and our hands were stretched forth in salutation. Even then his welcome was uttered with a half choked utterance,—his eye was fastened upon my face, even while he spoke to Ashley,—and I could not but think, from its peculiar expression, that he half divined the melancholy office on which I came. Seats were brought out into the piazza, and, motioning us to take them, the old man sunk into one himself,—not waiting for us,—as if in utter exhaustion.

" You seem feeble, Parson Potter,—you are not unwell, I hope;" said Ashley.

"No, I thank you—I am not unwell.   God has been merciful to me."

"I should think so; you are a pretty old man now."

"Ah! yes! old enough to be better."

"That may be said of the very best of us.   But let me introduce to you my friend, Mr. Clifton. You have already seen him, I think."

"Yes—I think I have—last night"— The tones and manner surprised us,—but the words more.

"Last night!" exclaimed Ashley."

"You forget, Sir," said I—"it was yesterday, when I lost myself hunting, and you were so good as to provide me with dinner, and direct me on my way."

He met what I said with a ghastly stare, but said nothing.   An unpleasant pause followed, broken at length, by Ashley, in the following manner.

"We never see you now, friend Potter.   Why is this.   Mrs. Ashley asks after you frequently— asks why I do not bring you frequently to dine with us, and will scarcely believe me, when I tell her that the fault is yours.   You must know that we should always be glad to see you."

"I thank you, Sir,—I thank you very much. You are too good.   But I am too old for much visiting.   I seldom go abroad.   My thoughts are pretty much with the dead.   I have little to do among the living, except to exhort them to better doings than my own."

This last sentence seemed to furnish an opening which was wanting. Ashley instantly said—

"Parson Potter, there is a little business about which we have come to see you, and I am glad that you seem in a proper frame of mind to attend to it. You once lived at my wife's place, Eagle-Ærie, I believe."

"Many years ago;" was the answer, in a deep sepulchral voice, as if requiring great effort.

"You *overseed* for her grandfather, the late Col. Hutchinson."

"I did, Sir."

"While there, you were, I believe, particularly unfortunate in your family—you lost your brother and wife, I think, in a very melancholy manner!"

For a moment or two no answer was given to this question. His face, meanwhile, underwent a change that was painful to behold. It was as if he had been struck with sudden idiocy. His features became suddenly expressionless. A vacant stare filled his eyes, which rolled from side to side, now on Ashley and now on myself. But, quite as suddenly, the vacancy cleared away. Intelligence seemed to return with the rapidity of a flash of lightning. He seemed as if just starting out of the profoundest sleep, into the most acute consciousness of life. He looked at us alternately, as if he knew all and foresaw all that we would say, then, passionately clasping his hands together, he exclaimed:—

"Gentlemen, what is it you would have? What would you know? What *do* you know? I see that you know something—speak—say! I am ready. I can bear to hear—nay, I am not afraid to speak. Only, of God's mercy, do not keep me in suspense. Let me hear the worst!"

His eye was now fixed on mine. I felt a stronger voice than his, within me, commanding me to speak, and speak boldly. I did so. I gave him a succinct narrative of all the experience which I had had at Castle Dismal, of the Haunted Chamber, and the mysterious Grove, in substance, as it has been already made known to the reader. He listened not in silence, but without a word. Deep groans burst from his lips at intervals, as I proceeded, and at the close, he exclaimed—

"It is done—it is fallen—the bolt has fallen! God's will be done! God's will be done!"

With these words, he fell forwards, prostrate, between Ashley and myself—his hands covering his face, and offering no effort to prevent his fall. We stooped to raise him, but found him in a swoon. Water was procured, and the usual means resorted to, for restoration, and our pains were rewarded,—though not for a considerable time—by a discovery of the signs of life. His eyes opened intelligently—he spoke—though his words were in a whisper.

"I understand—I know you!" he said, addressing me. "Wait awhile,—have patience, and I will be strong—strong enough for the rest."

A mattrass was brought from the house, upon which we laid him in the piazza. Water was given to him at his request, of which he drank copiously, though every now and then a spasm would almost force the vessel from his lips, and eject from his throat the mouthful that it held. It need not be said that we waited upon him patiently, and watched him tenderly. After a while he revived, sufficiently, as he himself insisted, to discourse to us freely upon the subject which had been so distressingly begun. But he deceived himself. His strength failed. His head was no sooner raised, than he showed symptoms of returning weakness. We discouraged his present attempts at speech, and counselled him to give himself rest. Another time would serve for his answer, and we promised to see him when he was better able.

" You are right," he said. " I thank you, gentlemen. Yet, before you leave me, it will be only proper to say that what Mr. Clifton has seen of me and mine—of my guilt and my agonies— is true. His thoughts of me are not always true, yet too nearly so. I slew not the wretched woman—the poor unfortunate—though my conscience rightly charges me with her death. Hand of mine hurt no hair upon *her* head ;—but I threatened it, and she feared it,—and perished through that fear. Enough now ;—I can no more !—Come to me again. To-morrow !—to-morrow !"

CHAPTER XVI.

THE STORY OF WILLIAM POTTER.

WE saw that no further progress was to be
made during that interview, and feeling that our
presence only served to keep the guilty man from
repose, we took our departure—"not standing
on the order of our going, but going at once."
We reached home at a tolerably late dinner hour,
and discussed, in unusual silence, the good things
of our hostess. She had her inquiries, of course,
but got no satisfaction. Still, we could not conceal that something had greatly interested, and
somewhat disturbed us. Our faces told tales, if
our lips did not, and subjected us accordingly to
a good deal of cross-examination, and some few
jeers, which we endured with christian fortitude.
Elizabeth Singleton was something graver than
usual, though she contrived at chess to deprive
me of my Queen in the most mortifying manner,
compelling an exchange, and giving me no better
equivalent, than a poor and no longer useful
Knight. As little can I say for my own knight-
hood that day—certainly nothing for my chivalry
as a Squire of Dames. True, I lingered by her
side—was interested in her presence—in what
she said and what she looked. But so far as conversation went, I might as well have been any

one of the hundred old trees about us, that every now and then, rattled their dry leaves against the panes. We separated for the night at an early hour, Mrs. Ashley making the movement, as I thought, with some precipitation,—being rather eager, as I fancied, to bring her husband to an early account of the mystery that troubled us. I did not suffer her to depart, however, without telling her, with some abruptness, that she must give me another chamber. The truth is that I shrunk from the idea of another night in the apartment which had hitherto accommodated me. I know no better reason for this change of feeling and resolve, than the simple fact that the assurances of William Potter, seemed to leave it no longer a matter of doubt that my visitations had been of a supernatural character. I suppose that one could only support the presence of an apparition by the lurking doubt, which must naturally prevail in every mind, whether or not it be one. Coleridge, by the way, has somewhere, some strong language upon this subject. He says that no man, seeing a ghost, and *knowing* it at the time to be such, could possibly survive it. I am not sure that I quote his remark literally, but it is substantially to this effect. I am not willing to subscribe entirely to this opinion. But this is not a place for the argument. It may be said, however, that assuming his own assertion, as a premise,—which is clearly against all rules of logic —making an inference usurp the place of a

8

groundwork,—he jumps to the farther conclusion, that there can be no ghosts. I need not say to the reader that this narrative alone is satisfactory on this subject; though, by this time, we doubt not that the author of the " Auncient Marinere," and " Christabel,"—who ought to be a believer, if any man—has been convinced by far higher authority.—Enough for the present that I had my chamber changed, and retired for the night with the comforting assurance that I should enjoy an uninterrupted time with Morpheus for the next ten hours.

I slept even longer, and rose to a late breakfast. I soon discovered from the guilty looks of Ashley, and the swelling glances of his wife, that he had been made to deliver up his secrets. Miss Singleton too had the appearance of one burdened by oppressive circumstances. Nothing, however, was said at breakfast on the subject. When this was over, Ashley went out to order our horses,—his wife followed him, and as I approached Miss Singleton, I was surprised to see her rise and advance to meet me with hand extended and eyes full of tears.

"Oh, Mr. Clifton," she exclaimed, " I have heard all of this dreadful story."

" Indeed."

" Yes, Mrs. Ashley has told me all, but though it be true, though William Potter has admitted the truth of all, yet I entreat you do not expose him farther—do not prosecute the matter against him. I will answer for it he is no criminal now, —but a good man, who has thoroughly repented of his sins. It can do no good now to bring him to justice. At his time of life it is better that he should be left to God. It will not be long before he is summoned to appear before the final Judge. Do not,—do not,—*you* appear against him,— spare him, in pity, I implore you."

This was not all said in a breath. Though earnest, the speaker was not vehement. Nay, she was subdued, nervous, and, though speaking, as we see, to the point, yet she trembled not a little, and faltered somewhat, and was agitated to a degree, which, I confess it, was not unpleasant to me to behold. Hitherto, Elizabeth Singleton had seemed to me rather an unimpressible, impracticable person. She was stately and calm, and if I may *now* declare so much, it did seem to me to be an objection to her, that she was not apt to show any of that incertitude of manner, that nervous fidgettiness, which, in a young lady, so far as it betrays an infamiliarity with the world, is a rather pleasing feature in the sight of a veteran like myself. Men do not usually admire ladies of that even and stately carriage, that cool and assured temper, which never suffers them to be taken by surprise ; and the high aristocratic training, and, I may add, temper, of Elizabeth Singleton, had rendered her very much a being of this description. I had overlooked the fact, which was also sufficiently known to my

experience, that it is very frequently the case
that the coldness and reserved loftiness of demeanor, of some persons, is nothing more than the
mask worn by the nicest and most trembling sensibilities ;—that, in this way, persons of the most
delicate mental and moral endowments seek to
protect themselves against invasion ; and, the
mask, become a habit, is too commonly confounded with the soul which it only serves to
shelter and conceal.   I must confess that the new
attitude in which I saw Elizabeth Singleton—
that of a pleader—was eminently gratifying to me.
She could feel—she could fear—she had sensibilities—she could tremble at their instance—the
woman had a girl's heart in spite of her *haut ton*.
What was more—her proceeding gave me an
advantage over her, of which the man-instinct, at
that moment, prompted me to take advantage.
I took her hand in mine, led her to a seat, and
we talked of William Potter, to be sure—but we
talked at the same time of other matters.   In
short, that hour saw all the hopes and schemes
of our hostess realized.   I made an avowal, and
she a confession, which—but Elizabeth Clifton,
who is at this very moment looking in upon me
from the piazza of our town house, can speak for
herself.   She is gone,—but, if you believe me,
stranger, that very lady was no long time since
the veritable Elizabeth Singleton, of whom we
have seen so much.

We made mutual promises, and, by this time,

Frank Ashley made his appearance, to say that the steeds were ready.

We heard nothing that day from William Potter. We concluded not to disturb him—not to hurry him. In truth, save for the gratification of a curiosity which was natural enough, we had no farther object in seeing him. I had promised Elizabeth Singleton not to annoy him, and, indeed, even if I had made no such promise, I could not have found it in my heart to take any farther steps in the business. It seemed to me as if I had done all that was required of me. My conscience was easy. Nay, what greater punishment could there be to a man, at his time of life, and in his situation, greater than the conviction that his crime was not in his own keeping. And what of that crime? Terrible as we might reasonably think it, had it not its own terrible provocation?—Hearing nothing then that day from William Potter, we concluded that he was still too feeble for an interview—for further communications. This too was natural and reasonable enough, and we reconciled ourselves to the prospect of delay, with our best reserves of patience and philosophy. We took for granted that the poor old man would keep his bed for a week or ten days at least. What then was our surprise, the next morning,—which was the Sabbath—to receive a message from him, informing us he was to preach that very day, at 12 M. at the Harmony Meeting House. We were astounded.

"Can it be that he will undertake to preach again—nay, that he can have the face, the strength for it?" exclaimed Ashley.

"We shall see. We must go."

"To be sure we must! at all events, if it be only to see how he can carry himself."

The ladies declared their purpose to go, as a matter of course, and we were on the road at the necessary hour. I may add, though the reader will scarcely consider this fact very important to the narrative, that, in spite of the sniggering of Frank Ashley, I took my seat in the carriage with Elizabeth. Until this time I had usually ridden on horseback. My notions in sundry maters, had evidently undergone a change.

———

A country church in South Carolina, need not be described. It is not customarily a very attractive building. Were we now writing of the old time parochial churches, built under British domination, something might be said, in relation to the massive, the picturesque, and the antique, which were to be found, combined in their structure or their adjuncts—ancient vault, quaint inscription, and shrouding, venerable oaks! But republicanism lacks reverence. We do not care a straw what sort of building we set aside for the Deity, and few of the country churches in the South—apart from the towns and villages—are quite so good as the barns of the neighboring planter. New Harmony Meeting-House was not much better than the majority. It was large enough for the congregation, and could yield shelter from the rain. It is not improbable too, that the words of truth and life—that is of God, who is both—were listened to, in that rude fabric, with quite as much attention as in St. Paul's or St. Peter's. Verily, the brick and mortar, though they make glorious religious buildings, do not wholly make the religion. Nay, exterior charms being wanting, may we not take for granted, that the impulse which brings the sinner to the miserable country church, is very like to be a religious one!

———

The congregation was a large one. The seats were all filled before the arrival of the parson. He, at length, made his appearance. We did not present ourselves at his approach, for fear of distressing him, but we could see him, where we stood, with ease and distinctness, and it did not escape us that a material change had taken place in his face and person in the last forty-eight hours. He seemed on a sudden to have sunk into imbecility. His form, very erect and massive when I had first seen him, was now bent and emaciated. His step, which, before, had been firm if not elastic, was now uncertain and feeble. His face had grown white and death-like, and the skin hung about his cheeks and chin in little sacks, which seemed crumpled and without vitality. But there was a remarkable brightness of his eye, which denoted the presence of active inner fires,—while the close compression of his thin lips was indicative of a stern decision of character, and a firmness of resolve, which seemed to have recently undergone close mental tasking, with the view to being properly confirmed and strengthened. I do not think he saw us at the time we made these observations. He walked directly from the humble vehicle in which he came to the church, accompanied by numbers of the male part of the congregation who had lingered without, in waiting for his arrival. From the studious deference of their approach and address, the solicitude with which they urged their inquiries as to his health,—it was evident that the venerable man was much beloved among them. My heart smote me as I watched the scene and thought how much I had contributed, perhaps vainly, not only towards disturbing his comfort, but the consideration which he held among his flock.

———

Having given him, as we thought, sufficient time to ascend the pulpit and take his seat, we entered the church, which was by this time so well filled that we had some little difficulty in procuring places. It was not until we were fairly seated that we discovered that Potter had not ascended the pulpit, but sat, to the evident astonishment of all persons, on one of the steps which led to it. His head was down, resting upon his palms—his face concealed, while his thin, long white hair, half covering his fingers,

was wet with the big drops of perspiration that
continued to rise upon his brow and roll off upon
his hands. It reminded me, not to be irreverent,
of the bloody sweat of the Saviour. It was the
mark of a great agony within. His spirit was
at strife with itself, and this show of mental
struggle tended somewhat to diminish those
doubts of the old man's virtue, which his resolution to preach had naturally awakened. In this
way he sat, neither lifting hand nor eye, until
sometime after the usual hour for commencing
the religious ceremonies of the day. At length,
a hymn given out by one of the elders aroused
him. The strain was sung in the simple touching style common to the Methodists ;—that style
which is so effective, poured forth among the hills
or the primitive forests, with the wild solemnity of
which it seems so happily to harmonize. When
this was over, the old man rose—a deep groan
breaking from his chest, evidently in spite of all
his efforts, as he looked round upon the congregation. He stood, where he had risen, silent, incapable, for a while, of utterance. But his looks,
meanwhile, were more eloquent than words.
They sufficiently said to all who saw them, that
something terrible was to be revealed—something
which might well justify the reluctance of the
lips to speak. At length the silence was broken.
The lips unclosed, and though the frame of the
speaker shook with his emotions, his words were
clear and full, and copious.

"Be not surprised, my brethren, that I do not
a*

ascend that sacred desk. I shall never again ascend it. It is my shame and my reproach that I
have so often dared, with the consciousness of
secret sin upon me, to defile its holiness with my
presence—to speak to you from its awful elevation,—in the dreadful presumption of heart which
made me, leprous as I am with evil deeds, undertake to expound the divine will, and stand up before you the representative of the Divine Presence.
Oh! beloved friends, forgive me that I have dared
so much. I may crave without sin for *your* forgiveness, for verily I have striven truly in *your*
behalf. But what will secure me the forgiveness
of God—what will save me from that curse of
presumption, which has hardened my heart against
the truth, and made me blind to the fearful arro-
gance with which I chose the profession of the
priest of God, before I was yet cured of the vilest
sins of the devil!

" Brethren, do not think me mad, or suffering
from any weakness of the brain, any wandering
of the intellect. I believe, from my soul, that
my mind was never calmer, never more free
from infirmity than it is at this moment. My
heart, too, was never in better state than at this
moment, and I may say to you, dearly beloved
brethren, that I never was more fit to go up into
that sacred place, than now, at this very moment,
when I feel and declare to you how impious it
was that I should ever have made bold to go
there. Yes, my brethren, if this day, I come before you to acknowledge my sins—sins of the most

heinous kind—sins of which none of you, perhaps, ever could have thought me guilty,—it is some consolation to me to feel that now, in the hour of my greatest unworthiness, God has been merciful to me,—has given me strength to make public my confession, and to take the first step towards throwing off the heavy chains of Satan.

"Oh, brethren! I have need of all your prayers. You see before you a man whose heart has been filled with crimes, whose hands have been stained by their performance,—and who has hushed his heart to silence when it would have spoken, and covered his hands so that its stains might not be seen,—and, knowing all his own guilt, has made bold to speak of yours,—to stand up here, for more than twenty years in the denunciation of the sinner, he, himself being the very worst among you. This, my brethren, is a shocking confession,—but as God hears me at this moment, it is a true one. It comes from the bottom of my soul,—yet the worst of it is, my brethren, that I have no merit for making this confession. It is forced from me. The finger of God laid bare my secret, and made it known by the most wonderful of his providences, before I had the courage or the truth, to come before you and acknowledge my own evil deeds and passions.`

" Let me ask my brethren, if Squire Ashley and his friend, be among you? I see them not."

He was answered. Ashley rose and made himself visible.

" I am glad," said the old man, in somewhat

lower tones.   Then addressing those occupying
the bench immediately before him, he proceeded:

"My brethren, suffer Squire Ashley and his
friend to be seated nigh me.   I know not if my
voice reaches them.   I know not if I shall have
the strength to make them hear me, and it is
needful that they in particular, should know the
truth.   It is through them, under God's will, that
I am brought, this day, to testify before you—to
acknowledge my secret sins, and implore your
prayers to the Throne of Grace, that I may be
strengthened to repentance."

A few moments sufficed to seat us before him.
He smiled upon me feebly but affectionately.   A
pause ensued, in which, from the abstract and
foreign expression of his eye, I conjectured he
was busy in seeking strength from prayer.   This
done he proceeded.

"Brethren, it is not known to all of you that
many years ago, and before I presumed to take
upon me,—thrice-dyed sinner that I was!—the
Divine mission—I was an occupant, in the humble
character of an overseer, of the estate of the late
Colonel Hutchinson, now in the possession of our
friend and neighbor, Squire Ashley.   When I was
but twenty-five years old, I was first employed to
attend this plantation. I was left in the sole charge
of it when Col. Hutchinson went to England, and
was continued in this charge long after he returned.   I was faithful to his interests, made him
good crops, and he seldom came upon the place
except for a month or two in winter, and never

interfered in any of my arrangements. In this way I lived for seventeen years, a single man, and to all appearances a happy one. But I was not happy. There were two things that finally came to trouble me. I had the misfortune to have a younger brother—a half brother—the son of my father by another mother. There were twenty years between us. He was a tall handsome youth,—some of you may remember him—but, he was also a very vicious one. He was idle in his habits, violent and reckless in his passions, a false speaker, a brutal swearer, and too frequently, at the tender age of twenty, drunken, with liquor, as a beast. I had done my best to reclaim him. I had counselled him like a brother—sent him to school—shared with him my little earnings, and tried, in all ways, to prove to him that I wished to love him, as the son of my father. Verily, my brethren, I did my best to love him. I needed somebody to love, and he, of all my family, was the only one whom God had left me to love. But this infatuated youth would not suffer me to love him. He resisted my efforts to teach or guide him—he scorned my counsel—fled from the school where I placed him—robbed the person with whom I found him employment—squandered, in the most brutal vices, the money which I gave him; and, in a fit of drunken brutality, smote me to the earth, even while I exhorted him, as if I had been a stranger and an enemy. He then disappeared from my sight, and for five years I was freed from his presence and his excesses. Of

his course I know but one thing, which I learned
by accident, that he had gone upon the high seas
as a common sailor.

"After his disappearance, I found myself more
than ever alone.   In spite of his misconduct and
excesses, he was dear to me, as he furnished
something to which I could attach myself—something upon which I could expend my cares.   I
needed something to love—some fond human
heart, to which I could link my own, and in whose
affections I could set my own to grow, both being
nourished at the same fountains.   In an evil hour,
I happened upon the woman who afterwards became my wife.   In a luckless mood and moment,
I fancied that she could supply this want.   She
was beautiful, and I was weak enough to confound beauty of face and form with beauty of
mind and spirit.   I was captivated by her
seeming sweetness of temper, pleased with her
girlish playfulness, yielding gentleness, and timid
fondness.   I was guilty of the equally great error
of marrying, at the age of forty-three, a girl of
sixteen.   This might not have been so great an
error, had she been but commonly endowed with
sense ; but in my passion for beauty, I had failed
to perceive the extreme childishness, the infantine
weaknesses, of the object of my passion ;—or if I
did perceive them, I set them down for simple
prettinesses that spoke quite as much for her innocence as for her youth.   Alas ! my brethren, I
deceived myself in everything.   She was not
only weak, but vicious,—not only foolish, but

treacherous, and I soon discovered that, instead
of marrying a support and a sympathy, I had
taken to my bosom one that received its warmth
but gave none in return—one upon whom I could
not rely—whose mind, dazzled by the most tran-
sient attractions, was easily persuaded to a neg-
lect of her most imperious as her most ordinary
duties. But these discoveries were not made on
the instant. I was slow to make them, as I was
too unwilling to lose the assurances of that love,
the possession of which had been so precious to
my hopes.

"I had not been long married when my brother returned from sea. In the long time of his
absence, I had forgotten his excesses. At least
the memory of them was softened, and I was
willing to forget them in the restoration of one who,
bound to me by nature, I had also been anxious
to attach to me by the superior ties of love. The
deportment of Charles Potter somewhat contributed to make me forget his follies. He had grown
a more cautious and prudent, if not a better man.
He approached me with deference and respect,
professed a hearty gladness at seeing me, which
touched my heart, and was received, as a brother
should have been received, into the bosom of my
family. Here he remained, off and on, for a
period of several months. He frequently ab-
sented himself for short periods, but did not seem
to engage in any business, and I deemed it a duty
to urge upon him the necessity of taking some
steps towards his personal and pecuniary inde-

pendence. I confess that I might not have been
prompted to this suggestion, however proper, but
that I was pained to perceive a somewhat peculiar and growing intimacy between him and my
wife, which, though in itself inoffensive, seemed to
indicate a very close understanding between them,
which did not comport with the relations of either
to myself. Whether I suffered my suspicions to
be seen, I cannot pretend to say, but the effect of
my suggestions was to send him away in a partial fit of anger, with the assurance that his shadow
should never again darken my door. Months
passed and I saw nothing of him, but an accident,
in the meantime, revealed to me that my wife saw
him frequently,—and I was at length stricken to
the soul with the conviction, that she had seen
him to my shame and to her eternal ruin.

"Oh, brethren, I will not enlarge on the agony
of soul which possessed me, when I first sunk under this conviction. I had surrendered all my
affections to this woman—I had given her my
whole full heart—I had no other object to love—
no object to divert mind or feeling, or to lessen,
for a single moment, her undivided influence over
both. I was stricken down, crushed, and, in one
night, the hairs upon my brow whitened as you
see them. They seemed to have had their roots
in my heart.

"But though I was crushed in heart, and blight-
ed in hope, I was not unmanned. I aroused all
my resolution, determined to detect and to punish
the guilty pair, at the moment when the detection

was complete. How I waited, how I watched—
with what patience, with what seeming calmness,
—I need not tell you. Let it suffice you that I
at last succeeded—that I followed the guilty woman from my chamber—that I surprised them in
their lewd embraces, and that Charles Potter
perished by my act, if not by my arm. He was
killed by a falling tree—this was the return of
the Coroner's inquest—but, until Providence deemed that it should be known to this gentleman, in the
most mysterious way—none knew that my arm
had prepared the tree, as a trap for the guilty brother, and for the no less guilty wife. My act pre
cipitated the tottering mass upon them, when their
lips were glued together in sinful union. I had
decreed that the same death should fall upon both,
but my plan failed in part. He, alone, perished.
How she escaped—by what miracle,—the great
Father of the Universe alone can tell!

"She escaped from that dreadful death only
to find another. Flying to the house, believing
that the death of her guilty lover was due to the
sudden but just judgment of God, I confronted
her with the truth. Nay, I did not stop at that.
In the exasperation and madness of my heart, I
threatened her life, and she fled again! I pursued her, but, as I hope to live hereafter, not with
any purpose of spilling more blood—of taking
another life. No! The dreadful crime which I
had already committed sunk deep into my soul,
filling it momently with horrors from which I
labored vainly to escape. In pursuing the un-

happy woman, I had no purpose beyond that of
securing her person, until soothed and quieted, I
could force upon her mind the necessity of keeping her own secret, and thus saving ourselves
both from equal shame. But, flying under the
cover of night, I failed to overtake her footsteps.
Vainly did I search the woods,—a search in
which I was assisted by one only of those who
now hear me. You, Ephraim Wilson—you
alone remember that search, for you were one
of those who shrunk not from my side in the day
of my trouble. You were the witness of all my
agonies and fears, but you little knew the whole
dreadful secret which had torn up my soul by
the roots."

"I remember, William Potter—I remember,"
was the response of the aged man to whom
his appeal was made. But he offered no further
interruption, and the speaker continued :—

"Three days after, she was found!—I was
terribly avenged! In her fright, perhaps in her
desperation, as fearing a worse destiny at my
hands, the waters of the river, swollen by a late
freshet, received her, and finally threw up her
unconscious body upon the sandflat which bears
her name! Thus perished the guilty—those
only by whom my shame was known—by whom
my guilt might have been conjectured. But, God
was above, my brethren,—God was above,—and
in his own good time, he has made it known to
others. He was not swift to vengeance—he was
slow. He has given me full time for repèntance

—full time—and, sinner as I am,—wilful and woful,—the guilt and the misery are mine, that I have not yet found healing at his hands.

" Brethren, believe not that I took pleasure in these crimes. Believe not that a vindictive passion for revenge prompted them. I was wronged and I was wretched, and in the first wild feeling of madness, occasioned by my wrong, I felt ready and anxious to slay the wrongdoer ;—but deeply did I repent me of the deed the moment it was done. Deeply then, and long afterwards, did I repent ; for, from that very moment, the furies of remorse fastened on my heart. They followed in my footsteps—they hung over my shoulder— they gave me no moment of repose. By day— by night—sleeping and waking—I was haunted by the aspects of my victims ; but my deadlier torments were at midnight—at the bitter dark hour of midnight, when the deed was done. Since that hour, my beloved brethren, each night have I been compelled to see and to share in that dreadful catastrophe. I lie down—I sleep in my own bed, and I waken in convulsions. Terrible throes shake my body—I am racked with deadly spasms—as if soul and body were torn asunder— and when my eyes open to consciousness, I find myself in the gloomy chamber at Squire Ashley's, where I then slept, and I see the unhappy woman whom I slew—I follow her footsteps—I detect her with my wretched brother beneath the tree —I pull down its tottering masses upon them —I see him perish, and I see her fly. And this, my brethren, is the vision which, nightly, I am compelled to behold, and which has haunted my miserable eyes from the dreadful hour when the deed was really done—now nearly thirty years ago. That I have not died under the agony— that I did not perish at the first sight of the awful spectacle—can only be ascribed to that mighty power which has decreed me this terrible ordeal,—it may be for the benign purpose of making it instrumental for my regeneration— which has decreed that I should nightly suffer agonies far beyond those of death, yet still survive—nay, my brethren, worst of all, survive in sin—torn with the pangs of hell, yet sustained by its pride, and wearing its garments of hypocrisy. For what, my brethren, was this service of God— professing God—which I undertook ?—this high bearing of virtue and faith, which could lead me to set myself up as a teacher of men—as a saviour of souls ?—My own soul being, as it is, blackened with its suppressed sins, and standing before you daily, clad in white to your eyes, while to my own all is black and spotted beneath ! Oh! my brethren, my worst sin of all has been that of this dreadful hypocrisy—this assumption of the guise and garments of an angel of light, when, in my own heart, I could not but feel that I was the secret servant of the devil !

"Oh, brethren, dear brethren, let me have your prayers. Verily, I need them all. My own have not availed me. My own strength was my weakness, and the occasion of my overthrow. Yet, do not think, my brethren, that I have consented to this long experience of sin, without a struggle. My struggles were constant, enforced so terribly as they have been by the dreadful ordeal, which I was nightly doomed to undergo. I toiled to be good, to do good, to beat down evil, to speak well of my neighbor, to succor him in the moment of need, to sit beside him in his suffering, to cheer him in his despondency, and to open the way for him, which I had not found for myself, to the mercies of God, and the Eternal life of blessedness which is promised us in Jesus. You will all bear me testimony how faithfully I have done these things. But, alas! the best moments of my well-doing were clouded by the conviction of my own unexpiated, unacknowledged crimes. When I was enjoying the praises of good works on earth —enjoying your love and veneration, and secure in the affections of my flock,—my heart smote me with its secret undesert. Here was I, a criminal, a manslayer—like Cain,—the murderer of my brother—the murderer of all who were dear to me—living in high honor, on the fatness of the land, and glorying, as a man of mark and of substance! I craved religion—it was my prayer and my hope—truly did I feel that, unless I secured this blessing, all was nothing,—and yet, my brethren, I had not the courage to give up your favor—to incur your reproach—to lose the pleasant sunshine of your smiles, and the good favor in which you held me. My pride of heart—O! pride of Satan—would not suffer me to incur this

forfeiture, though, in place of it, there were vouchsafed me, in the future, the smiles of saints and
angels, the approval of all good spirits, "well
done" of God the Father, and his blessed Son,
our Saviour, evermore !

But brethren, what my feeble vanity and world-
ly pride would not suffer me to do, God has done by
other means. By a most wonderful providence, he
has revealed the story of my sin. He has shewn to
the eyes of the stranger, even as it was committed, the crime which has stained my hands and
my soul with blood. These nightly trials have
not been taken solely for my regeneration. The
torturous repetition of my evil deeds, recurring
as they have done punctually, each night, for the
long and dreary period,—even from that which
beheld them in reality,—have had in view my
detection and punishment. The object is at last
attained. There is a witness before me who will
tell the rest—who will relate to you his own discoveries. He has been chosen, as I consider
him, the instrument of Providence, for ending
these trials, and for avenging the long-defrauded
justice of the land. I bow with submission to
God's will. I am ready to submit ! Oh ! brethren, forgive me—pray for me—I have loved you,
and I love you still. I have worked in your behalf with truth and diligence. Had I but worked
only half so diligently in my own ! But I yield
myself. I am resigned. Father, be merciful—
be merciful !—Lord Jesus, have mercy upon me,
have mercy upon me !"

He descended as he spoke, from the slight elevation which he had occupied while speaking. His last words were uttered in choking accents, and the ghastliness of death overspread all his features. His eyes were bloodshot, but, unlike the eyes of all his flock, were without a tear. He tottered forward in the direction of my seat. His glance, which was glazed and inexpressive, was yet fixed upon me. It had a strange and painful expression. As he approached me, he spoke,—addressing me—his words now being incoherent and broken,—uttered spasmodically, and only after great effort.

"I am ready," he said. "I am ready. I oppose no resistance. I know that I have to die. The law must take its course. I have offended. I have offended. Minister of God's vengeance! To you I yield me! I am here! lead me! Let the executioner come!"

He extended his hands together, very much in the attitude of one who was expecting manacles, and thus speaking and acting, fell suddenly forward upon the bench where Ashley and myself were sitting—falling between us,—and, so suddenly, as to carry us all over with the shock. The bench was crushed. We leapt to our feet, and proceeded to raise him. But he gave us no assistance. The paroxysm was his last. He was dead—the victim of long repressed passions and fears, suddenly breaking all bounds, and stifling the feebler energies at last, by which they had so long been controlled and commanded!

*   *   *   *   *   *   *   *

We forbear all judgment upon his offences.
That he was more sinned against than sinning,
most readers will be ready to say with us.   That
he attached an unjust character to his assumption of the ministry—acting the part, as he had
done, with so much purity and humility—we
have no question.   The notion which he entertained that he was bound by religious principle
to make confession of his crime to man, as well
as to God, is one which few moralists will insist
upon.   His errors of opinion in this respect, and
the sufferings which he endured in consequence,
were no doubt the result of a delicate nervous
organization—such persons being very apt to
confound the sensibilities of temperament with
those of conscience.   But what shall we say of
these nightly struggles, in which he found himself borne back irresistibly to the scene of his
misdeeds and misfortunes ?   And what shall we
say of the ghostly visitations of Castle Dismal ?
The sceptic will smile, as before.   But this gives
us no concern.   Our purpose is not to overcome
the credulity of self-conceit, or inspire anew the
terrors of the credulous.   We couch ourselves
behind the refuge of Hamlet :—

> " There are more things in heaven and earth, Horatio,
> Than are dreamt of in your philosophy."

THE END.

www.ingramcontent.com/pod-product-compliance
Lightning Source LLC
Chambersburg PA
CBHW030824020726
47499CB00006B/2057